"You flatter yourself."

"I couldn't be interested in a man who holds me captive," Linden continued.

Steed's laughter mocked her. "Oh, Linden, you don't fool me for an instant."

"No," Linden said shakily, sounding far less certain than she would have wished. "It isn't what I want at all."

Steed's lashes dropped, hooding his derisive expression. "Liar," he taunted softly. "It is what you want, and sooner or later you'll be forced to admit it."

Valerie Parv was a successful journalist and nonfiction writer when she began writing for Mills & Boon in 1982. Born in Shropshire, England, she grew up in Australia and now lives with her cartoonist husband and their cat—the office manager—in Sydney, New South Wales. She is a keen futurist, a "Star Trek" enthusiast, and her interests include traveling, restoring dollhouses and entertaining friends. Writing romance novels affirms her belief in love and happy endings.

Books by Valerie Parv

A Reluctant
Attraction
Valerie Parv

Harlequin Books

TORONTO • NEW YORK • LONDON
AMSTERDAM • PARIS • SYDNEY • HAMBURG
STOCKHOLM • ATHENS • TOKYO • MILAN
MADRID • WARSAW • BUDAPEST • AUCKLAND

ISBN 0-373-17314-8

A RELUCTANT ATTRACTION

First North American Publication 1997.

Copyright © 1995 by Valerie Parv.

CHAPTER ONE

IF THE weather had matched Linden Taylor's mood, storm clouds would have overtaken the impossible blue of the sky and rain would have lashed the outback community of Derby on the Kimberly coast of Western Australia.

Contrarily the blazing sunshine mocked her annoyance as she confronted the butler whose burly form barred the entrance to the imposing Harbour Master's residence. Butler her eye! If the bulge under his jacket hadn't been enough, his hulking build would have marked him as a security man straight away.

She drew herself up to her full one hundred and seventy centimetres in height, well aware that the man's two-metre stature gave him the advantage. 'If Greg Hamil hears that you refused me admittance, it could cost you your job.'

As bluffing went it was a brave attempt. Greg didn't even know she was outside and he certainly hadn't invited her to his party. Deciding to come anyway had taken all her courage, but it was the only way to get the explanation he owed her.

The butler was unimpressed by her threat. 'I'm sorry, miss, my instructions are to admit only the invited guests.'

She hefted a wrapped parcel under his nose. 'Why would I bring a gift if I didn't know it was Greg's thirtieth birthday party?'

Under the guard's assessing eye she tried to project innocence through her dove-grey eyes. A thatch of curly blonde hair and a petite figure made her look younger than her twenty-five years, but it didn't help. 'You could have read about the party in the papers.'

It was so close to the truth that she stifled a gasp. She *had* read about the party only days after Greg had vanished from her life with no apology or farewell. Still, she hadn't intended to gatecrash the affair until his continued elusiveness drove her to it. This wasn't working either. Maybe she should give up and go home.

No, a defiant inner voice asserted. All her life she'd accepted being the one left behind but not this time. At the least, Greg owed her an explanation for letting her think he cared, then abandoning her. She forced a smile. 'I've just arrived in town so there probably wasn't time to get my invitation out.' Warming to her task, she leaned closer. 'In Perth, Greg and I were...well, you know how it is?'

'Just how is it?' drawled a challenging male voice.

Startled, she spun around, dropping the parcel which was deftly caught by the man standing behind her. He was close enough for her to feel his breath on the side of her neck. Involuntarily she sucked in air and her nostrils filled with a tantalising musky scent. Instantly her senses spun. Either he was wearing the world's most seductive aftershave lotion or his own male aura ought to be bottled for sale to the lovelorn.

He was taller even than the security man—er, butler—and his masculinity was just as devastating for being less overt. An impression of craggy features, a spare, muscular build and deep-set eyes gazing deeply into hers flashed through her mind.

She had her reaction under control within seconds although she felt as if she'd been staring at the man for an eternity. Eyes the colour of warm toffee met her startled gaze unwaveringly. 'You were saying?'

'I—er—thanks for catching my parcel. It's fragile.'

Ignoring the designer wrapping, he inspected the handwritten card. 'To dear Greg with love from Linden.' Coldness invaded his features. 'You, I take it, are Linden.'

'Yes.' She resisted the urge to snatch the parcel back. A tussle would only make her look worse in front of the security guard who was still her biggest obstacle to seeing Greg again. 'May I have my gift back?'

One dark eyebrow lifted ironically, giving the man's face a fleetingly satanic look which somehow matched the barely leashed energy in his powerful frame. 'I could give it to Greg for you.'

Although he reminded her of a cowboy from an old western movie, he wore the white shirt, figured tie and dark trousers which passed for formal attire in the tropics. 'You're going to the party?'

'Eventually.' Impatience radiated from every lithe line of his body.

'I didn't mean to delay you, but I really must see Greg myself.'

An eyebrow arched. 'He invited you to come?'

She shifted from one foot to the other. 'Not specifically. He didn't know I'd be in town. You see, we went out together in Perth and...well...'

'I know how it is.' He echoed her words, managing to load them with enough innuendo to fill a gossip column.

Annoyance flared through her. Who did he think he was anyway? 'You needn't make it sound so horrible. We saw quite a lot of each other in Perth and I decided to fly up and surprise him.'

'He'll be surprised all right,' he murmured.

'What do you mean?' He made it sound as if the surprise would be less than welcome. 'Greg suggested I should visit the Kimberley sometime.'

'"Sometime" is hardly specific. Lots of people issue casual invitations and don't expect them to be taken up.'

Something about the man's cool self-assurance struck sparks of response deep inside her and she flashed back, 'You'd be an authority, I suppose.'

Flames of response leapt in his dark gaze. 'Not at all. If I'd invited you to Derby, you'd be in no doubt that I meant it. Not only would a limousine have collected you from home and whisked you to Perth airport, but a private plane would have brought you to my side.'

The picture he painted brought a lump to her throat. What would it be like to be so cherished? 'Maybe I don't care for being wrapped in cotton wool,' she denied with less than absolute honesty.

His piercing glare recognised the lie for what it was. 'Not cotton wool. I prefer my women in silk and velvet,' he went on. 'But it wouldn't end with the journey. Another car, air-conditioned against the tropical heat, would bring you to the wharf where my cruiser would be waiting. The champagne would be chilled, a lobster or two prepared by way of refreshment, and in my stateroom——'

'Stop this.' She covered her ears as her mind raced ahead to the inevitable next stage of the fantasy. 'Why are you doing this?'

'To show you how different it is to be welcomed and truly desired.'

'What makes you think Greg won't welcome me?' She felt her face redden at the implication that her association with Greg paralleled the fantasy version.

'Your presence here on his doorstep. Admit it, Linden. You read too much into an offhand invitation.'

'I'll admit no such thing until I've talked to Greg and sorted out this misunderstanding. So give me my gift back. I'll present it to him when there aren't so many *obstacles* in the way.' Her furious look encompassed the security guard and this arrogant stranger with his all too beguiling fantasies.

His long fingers tightened around the parcel. 'Not so fast. Perhaps you should come to the party after all. It may save us all a lot of trouble later on.'

Why did she have the feeling there was more to his offer than generosity? She shot a sidelong glance at the guard, who was studiously ignoring the exchange. 'How can I? As you pointed out, I'm not on the guest list, although I'm not lying about knowing Greg.'

'But I *am* on the list and my invitation includes a friend.'

Presumably a lady friend, she thought, and was caught off guard by feelings of anger. She blamed it on disgust at the idea of being lumped in with his many conquests. 'I suppose you need me to save you from the embarrassment of arriving alone,' she ventured, unable to disguise a note of satisfaction.

His eyes darkened ominously. 'Arriving with you poses more problems than if I attend solo. The wording on the invitation is a product of my dear cousin's wishful thinking.'

'Greg is your cousin?'

Did she detect a flicker of distaste on his face? 'No, my cousin is our hostess, Sandra Cochran.'

It was the first she'd heard of Sandra Cochran. Maybe she was a maiden aunt of Greg's. He hadn't talked much about his private life, preferring to encourage Linden to talk about herself. She knew Greg's family owned a conglomerate of businesses in the north-west, but that was all. 'I don't know Sandra Cochran,' she mused aloud.

'I'll bet you don't.' The man's rapier tone sliced through her denial. 'But it's high time you did. Come with me.'

His grip on her arm gave her little alternative. Together they mounted the steps to a wide veranda which shaded a magnificently restored colonial mansion.

This time the guard didn't consult his guest list, she noticed. He merely sketched a salute in the air with his index finger and stood aside to admit them. Her curiosity increased. Who was her new-found escort?

As they were about to go inside she checked him. 'Shouldn't we introduce ourselves if we're supposed to be together?'

'It's purely a matter of convenience,' he said coldly, but added, 'Steven Dare. Steed to my friends.'

'Then I'd better call you Steven, hadn't I?' she rejoined angrily, already wishing that she'd stuck to her guns and tried to see Greg another time. If she hadn't experienced such difficulty in contacting him she wouldn't have been forced to gatecrash his party.

'Calling me Mr Dare would rather blow your cover, wouldn't it?'

Her cover? He was the one who needed a date to keep his macho image intact. 'I don't need a cover, as you call it,' she denied. 'I simply need to see Greg and sort a few things out.'

Things like why he had suggested she visit Derby if he didn't really mean her to come. She'd tried telephoning him from Perth but he had ended the call quickly, pleading a business commitment. She hadn't been able to contact him since she'd arrived three days ago. She hated to think that Steven Dare was right and the invitation had been a polite fiction all along.

It didn't fit in with the man who had wined and dined her so lavishly in Perth. At their first meeting, a fund-raiser for the centre where she worked as a sleep therapist, he had made no secret of his interest in her. Not only had he pressed her to go out with him, he had spent several nights at the centre, observing her work.

No man had ever wooed her so assiduously and she couldn't deny that she'd found it intoxicating. After being raised in a succession of group homes, she'd found it flattering to be pursued by someone as sophisticated as Greg Hamil.

All the same she had agonised over whether to accept his invitation to spend a weekend aboard his cruiser off Fremantle, being fairly sure what sort of weekend he'd had in mind.

Intimacy itself hadn't been the problem so much as her own uncertainty as to where the relationship was leading. The dilemma had solved itself, however, when she'd come down with a cold and couldn't go sailing at all. Unfortunately Greg had taken off back to Derby before he could repeat his invitation. If he intended to repeat it, she thought restively. It was one of the things she meant to find out today.

'Steed, you made it after all and you brought a friend along. Terrific.'

'Sandy, this is Linden from Perth. Linden, our hostess, Sandra Cochran.'

All thoughts of maiden aunts fled at the sight of the vivacious redhead who threw herself into Steven's arms and kissed him enthusiastically. Her green eyes sparkled with pleasure as she surveyed her cousin who had managed adroitly to disguise the fact that he didn't know his 'friend's' full name.

Linden framed a taut smile. 'It's nice to meet you, Sandra.'

She was uncomfortably aware of the speculative looks that Sandra darted her way as she and Steven exchanged family news. Belatedly he remembered his role as her escort and dropped his arm around her shoulder. 'We mustn't keep you from the party, Sandy. I'll look after Linden.'

His cousin's smile broadened. 'It doesn't look like a great hardship.'

'I couldn't agree more.' His fingers curled around the tendrils of hair at Linden's nape. It was a masterly touch, suggesting a greater intimacy than if he'd made a grander gesture. The light touch sent shivers scooting along her spine as if he'd sent a Morse code message all the way to her brain. Her startled gaze flew to his face, then she realised that the message was for his cousin's benefit. Too bad that the knowledge came a split-second after her body reacted to his touch by trembling uncontrollably.

On the pretext of admiring the hand-painted ceiling, she slipped away from him before she betrayed herself any further. This situation might be convenient for them both but she didn't want it getting out of hand. Coming to the party on his arm was all very well to get her through the front door but there it had to end.

'How is the birthday boy?' she asked Sandra grimly.

Sandy's smile faltered momentarily. 'Do you know Greg?'

'I've been telling Linden about him,' Steven said before she could utter a sound. 'We brought him a present.' He proffered Linden's parcel, the tag somehow ending up clinging to his palm, she noticed furiously. What was going on here?

The other woman's smile resumed its brilliance. 'Another gift? You're spoiling him. I'll put it with the others while you two make yourselves at home.'

Alone with Steven, Linden rounded on him. 'So "we" brought the present, did we? It would serve you right if it contained edible underwear.'

Her anger left him unmoved. 'You said it was fragile so I'm betting on men's toiletries. By the time he gets around to opening his gifts he'll have forgotten who it came from.'

'Which is the whole idea, isn't it?' she fumed. 'I saw you remove the tag, Mr Sleight-of-Hand. What I don't understand is what you're up to.'

'Are you forgetting you're supposed to be with me?'

'We only came through the front door at the same time. I am not *with* you.'

His eyes turned glacial. 'Would you prefer me to tell our friend at the door how recently we became acquainted?'

The result of such an action was entirely predictable. 'I either pretend to be with you or get myself thrown out, do I?'

'It's your choice.'

It was like choosing between the proverbial rock and the hard place but there was really no alternative if she wanted to see Greg. She hadn't realised how difficult it would be to get in touch with him. His wealth created barriers she hadn't anticipated, such as the over-sized butler guarding the front door. 'You win,' she sighed.

He nodded grimly. 'I usually do.'

'But only until I've had a chance to see Greg.'

'It may take a while. Half the population of the north-west is here today.'

The wealthy half, she thought as they began to circulate.

Assuming she would have the best chance of being admitted without an invitation if she dressed for the occasion, she had chosen a fashionable knitted dress with a draped halter-top and sashed waist. The white fabric clung to her slim figure, the jewel neckline dipping to a draped back. The hemline just grazed her knees.

The dress had cost her most of a week's salary but she still felt under-dressed alongside the other women. Although most wore casual attire she recognised several designer labels and enough gemstones to stock a small jeweller's shop. She felt her first serious twinge of unease. Perhaps Greg hadn't invited her in case she was out of place.

As they moved slowly through the throng it became obvious that Steven was well-known. As he introduced her she heard her name repeated so many times that she wondered if he was deliberately trying to overwhelm her with new faces.

His hold on her arm was so tenacious that she had no choice but to remain at his side or risk creating an undignified scene if she tried to break free.

Finally he found them a quiet corner and a glass of champagne. 'Aren't you carrying this togetherness act a bit far?' she asked as the drink cooled her parched throat. 'How will you explain it when I vanish from your life as suddenly as I appeared?'

His eyes challenged her over the rim of his glass. 'I never explain myself to anyone. Besides, you haven't vanished yet.'

She set her glass down on a side-table. 'But I intend to as soon as I've sorted things out with Greg.'

His gaze became hooded. 'You seem sure things will work out to your satisfaction. Surely if he wanted to see you he would have done so by now?'

The possibility had nagged at her since she'd spoken to Greg on the phone but pride wouldn't let her admit it to an arrogant brute like Steven Dare. 'He's a busy man—he may not have had time.'

'A man can always make time for a beautiful woman,' Steven drawled silkily.

'I suppose you don't think I'm beautiful enough for him to bother about,' she challenged, foolishly hurt by the insinuation.

'On the contrary, I think you're beautiful enough for any man to bother about.' She tensed as his finger grazed the side of her face then travelled along her jawline to skim the pulse-point hammering crazily at her throat.

She reared away as if stung. 'Don't. Everyone's looking at us.'

He preferred to continue his slow appraisal of her face, feature by feature. 'Let them look.'

This was insane. She had agreed to accompany him to gain admission, not to get involved with him. She was here to see Greg, but Steven was confusing the issue. He had stretched an arm across her shoulder, resting his hand on the massive colour-stone fireplace.

The gesture created an island of intimacy around them. Had she really been his partner it would have thrilled her, but they were strangers, although he refused to act like one. The broad expanse of his chest brushed the points of her breasts through the knitted fabric, chafing them unbearably. His breathing remained slow and even in contrast to her increasingly shallow gasps as he deliberately narrowed the gap between them. She flattened her palms against his chest but it was like trying to hold back one of the Kimberley's notorious king tides. She felt as overwhelmed as if he *were* the tide, sweeping her out of her depth into an emotional abyss which was beyond her experience.

What was happening to her? Her heart trip-hammered in her chest and her tongue darted out to moisten parched lips. At the gesture she saw his throat tighten. So he wasn't as impassive as he appeared. It was as if the world had telescoped until there were only herself and Steven in it. She had never felt so aware of a man before.

A flurry of activity across the room broke the spell and she dragged her eyes away from Steven, refocusing with difficulty. 'Greg's coming this way.'

'So?'

'So let me pass. This may be my only chance to see him.'

'Uh-uh.' Unbelievably his arm snaked around her waist and he pulled her against him. The cry of protest she summoned never escaped her throat because it was silenced by the compelling pressure of his mouth against her own.

Shock made her part her lips, unwittingly abetting the plunder of her emotions. Her head swam and her throat ached with the need to order an end to the conflicting messages that her senses were receiving. She certainly didn't want him to kiss her, so why were her pulses keeping time with the beat of his heart she could feel under her palm?

Powerless to free herself, she was forced to cling to him or crumple to the floor. Time stood still as he prolonged the moment, drawing his mouth away from hers only with seeming reluctance when Greg was almost upon them.

Her eyes spat flame as she opened her mouth to vent her rage at Steed for taking such blatant advantage of her. But she was not to be allowed the satisfaction of calling him the names that her outrage conjured up. Keeping his arm around her waist, he acknowledged Greg's arrival with a nod. 'Ah, the man of the hour.'

Greg's eyes had narrowed as he'd approached but she could swear she saw relief in them at the sight of her in Steed's arms. 'Man of the hour, but obviously not of the moment.'

Steed's abashed look went nowhere near his eyes. 'I'm sure you know how it is.' There was deliberate mockery in his use of Linden's own phrase, and amusement in the look he directed at her, obviously for Greg's benefit.

Greg nodded hearty agreement—too hearty, Linden thought. Surely he should be annoyed to find her in his friend's arms? 'This isn't what you think,' she began.

Greg waved away her denial. 'What I think doesn't matter, Linden. I'm delighted you didn't come all this way just to renew a business acquaintance with me. I hope you continue to have a wonderful stay.'

A business acquaintance? Linden almost choked on the flagrant lie. Granted, they had met in a business setting, but everything afterwards had been strictly personal, or so Greg had let her think.

'You're a dark horse, Dare,' Greg commented. 'How long has this been going on?'

Clamping her mouth shut, Linden let Steed answer. With any luck, if she gave him enough rope he would hang himself. She should have known better. 'I've had my sights on Lin since I first set eyes on her,' he rejoined without missing a beat.

'So you've known each other for a while?'

'We've only just——'

'Only just realised what's happening,' Steed cut in, once more leaving her speechless with annoyance. She had never disliked anyone as much as she hated Steven Dare at that moment. Greg had only to look at her furious expression to see the truth but it seemed he was happy to accept Steven's explanation. In fact, she had a suspicion that he was clutching at it like a lifeline.

He patted her arm distractedly. 'Enjoy the party.' Then he was gone, swallowed up by the crowd.

She tried to pull away but Steed's grip tightened. 'You're not going anywhere.'

It was as if he'd clamped a girdle of steel around her waist. 'Let me go or I'll——'

'You'll what? Scream? Cry rape? After being seen melting in my embrace, how much credibility do you think you'll have?'

'You did it on purpose,' she railed at him, her tone vibrant with fury. 'You deliberately let Greg think we're involved.' The very thought sent a shudder down her spine. 'All that nonsense about having your eye on me since you first saw me— which was about an hour ago at the most.'

His gimlet gaze transfixed her. 'That's where you're wrong. I was in Perth on business during the last couple of months, ample time to see what you were up to. I didn't think you'd have the nerve to show up here today of all days.'

Her thoughts spun dizzily. What had she and Greg done together to earn his derision? He had spent a couple of nights observing her work but Steed couldn't possibly be aware of those. They had barely even kissed until the night Greg had tried to persuade her to spend a weekend aboard his boat.

She thought frantically. Granted, their meetings had been in out-of-the-way places, but this was to avoid the prying eyes of the media, Greg had assured her. Given his family's high profile, this was understandable. She too would hate to be the focus of tabloid gossip writers.

For the same reason she had agreed to pose as Greg's secretary when she'd gone with him to inspect apartments in the city. The estate agent had had no idea how Linden fantasised about the flat as their shared home.

Greg's prudence had been vindicated when they'd dined at a tiny French restaurant. As they were leaving, Greg had spotted a reporter from the society pages. Giving her the money to pay for their meal, Greg had slipped out a back way, instructing her to meet him there after he brought the car around.

They had laughed about such escapades, feeling like schoolchildren with a delicious secret. She had been in no hurry for Greg to make their romance public if it meant sharing him with news-hungry journalists.

Had Steven seen them together and decided there was something amiss in their behaviour? If so, it was too bad. She had done nothing to be ashamed of. 'It's hardly your business what I do,' she reminded him.

He seemed to reach a decision. 'How much?'

'What?'

'Whatever Greg was paying for your services, I'll double.'

The offer took several seconds to reach her stunned brain but her reaction was instantaneous. Her open palm connected with the side of his face almost before she knew what she meant to do. As she stared at the imprint of her hand fading from his cheek, horror welled through her. She had never done such a thing before, even under extreme provocation, but now she had lost control in front of Steven Dare. She wanted the floor to open up and swallow her.

His eyes were unreadable and his expression stony, but a muscle worked revealingly along his jaw. Nevertheless his control was masterful.

Gathering the shreds of her poise, she whirled around, seeking the sanctuary of a bathroom she had glimpsed on the way in. Steed didn't move but she felt his eyes following her with the intensity of laser beams, every step of the way as she retreated.

CHAPTER TWO

SLUMPED against the expansive marble vanity, she fought for composure. Steven Dare thought that Greg had paid for her company. How could he think such a thing?

Then she recalled helping Greg shop for an apartment, and the times he'd given her money to pay for things while he stayed in the background. How had it looked from a distance?

If only she'd been able to see Greg first, he would have explained everything then Steven could choke on his vile suspicions.

The door opened behind her and she dug into her bag for her make-up as Sandy Cochran joined her and began to fuss with her hair. 'Enjoying the party?' she asked, comb poised in mid-air.

'Yes, thank you.' She hid her expression behind a tube of lipstick.

'I'm so glad you came with Steed. From the way he acts around you it seems he's already smitten.'

The lipstick ground against Linden's teeth and she blotted it with a tissue. 'I'm not sure "smitten" is the right word.'

'Believe me, I know Steed. I lived with his family after my parents died when I was eleven so he's more like a brother than a cousin to me. I was hoping some woman would come along and lure him away from those outback expeditions of his. He's been alone for too long.'

With a bright smile she left and Linden stared at her startled expression in the mirror. Outback expeditions? He was *that* Steven Dare, author of countless books about the outback and maker of documentary films of his expeditions. She was surprised she hadn't recognised him on sight, except that he looked more civilised here than on television where he frequently sported a beard.

All the same, his being famous didn't give him the right to slander her good name. He might look civilised but his behaviour towards her was barbaric.

Head high, she sailed out of the ladies' room determined to avoid him at all costs. But she got no further than the hallway, where he lounged indolently, obviously waiting for her to emerge.

'Can't let her out of your sight for a minute, can you, Steed?' another guest joshed.

Steed threw the man a fraternal look. 'Can you blame me?'

'Stop this,' she grated, not caring if anyone overheard. 'Now I know what you think of me, I'm surprised you want to be seen with me at all.'

He ran his fingers along his cheek. 'Obviously some of my information was off target, unlike your right arm.'

She blinked back tears of frustration. 'What you as good as called me isn't in the least amusing. Well, you've had your fun, Mr Dare, and now I'm leaving.'

His gaze hardened. 'Without getting what you came for? I was about to take you back to Greg.'

If only Greg would explain who she was and how they met. Watching Steven Dare eat his words would be a pleasure. 'Now?' she said disbelievingly.

'Right now.' He caught at her wrist. 'There's something you ought to know first.'

She tugged impatiently at his arm. 'Whatever it is, it can keep.'

'Suit yourself.'

He gave in rather too easily, she thought suspiciously as he led her to a reception-room where a small podium had been set up. Most of the guests were clustered around it. She caught a glimpse of Greg standing behind an older man who was making some sort of announcement.

'So I'd like you to join me in toasting the happiness of my son, Greg, and his lovely bride-to-be, Sandra Cochran.'

Sandra Cochran was going to marry Greg? The truth blinded Linden with its obviousness. Sandra's almost incandescent happiness, Greg's reluctance to see her. Why hadn't she realised? No wonder Steed couldn't wait to see her reaction to his bombshell.

She felt as if the floor had begun to tilt under her. Someone thrust a glass of champagne into her hand and she spilled it with the force of her trembling.

It was becoming clearer now. The way Greg had chosen to meet her in out-of-the way restaurants and on his boat, blaming snoopy press photographers for his reticence. His eagerness to pair her off with Steed. All he'd wanted was an affair before his marriage.

Steed's voice penetrated her confusion. 'I'll drive you home. Where are you staying?'

'There's no need. You've achieved your aim now.'

He ignored this. 'Where are you staying?'

Since he wasn't about to give up she gave him the name of the apartment block where she'd rented a flat for a month. How naïvely optimistic it seemed now. She could hardly believe she'd been so blind. Greg must have been mortified when she'd actually turned up. No doubt he'd trusted that Derby was sufficiently far from Perth for her never to take him up on his blithe invitation.

She was hardly aware of being steered to a Range Rover and settled into the front passenger seat.

'I suppose you're happy now, having saved your cousin from the predatory city female? Well, don't expect any thanks from me. You set me up in there.'

He changed gears with an aggressive action. 'I don't expect your thanks, but I do expect your co-operation.'

Confusion piled on confusion. 'What do you mean?'

'You may or may not be the innocent party here, but Sandra Cochran certainly is. She may have lousy taste in men but she's the nearest thing I've got to a sister and I won't allow you to hurt her. So forget any notion of causing trouble between her and Greg Hamil or you'll have me to answer to. Is that clear?'

'It's clear enough.' She bit her lower lip to hold back the tears. She was damned if she'd cry in front of him. Her only satisfaction was in knowing that she would never have to see him again after today.

She directed a sidelong look at his finely chiselled profile, unwillingly recalling the way his kiss had burned on her lips. Now he looked infuriatingly self-assured. 'You're enjoying this, aren't you?' she flung at him.

He nodded tautly, his eyes fixed on the road. 'It gives me some satisfaction to see you paid back in your own coin.'

She writhed against the confining seatbelt. Had the car been stationary she would have jumped out and left him to his unsavoury thoughts. Since she couldn't she decided to fight back. 'Hadn't you better say what you mean?'

His long fingers flexed around the steering-wheel as if he would prefer them to be around her throat. 'Do I need to spell it out? From the moment you met Greg Hamil you've had your eye on the main chance. Why else would you transplant yourself over two thousand kilometres on the strength of an offhand invitation? The apartment you've taken has a minimum rental period of a month so you obviously plan to stick around.'

She wasn't about to tell this arrogant, unfeeling man the real reason why she had come to Derby. In any other circumstances she would have made sure of her welcome before booking her flight north. But she had needed the break and joining Greg here had seemed like the perfect solution to everything.

'How can you be so sure Greg's invitation was offhand?' she asked in a deliberately chilly tone.

'I know Greg. Ever since Sandy foolishly decided that he was the man for her, I've heard rumours about his extra-curricular activities. On my trip south I decided to find out the truth for myself.'

'And you saw us together and made up your mind that I was some sort of scarlet woman.'

'According to my sources, Hamil wasn't too choosy about the kind of women he saw, and I was determined to protect Sandra. Nevertheless, I almost convinced myself you were an innocent.'

Her chin lifted. 'Were, past tense? What changed your mind?'

'A talkative estate agent who sold Greg an apartment. Or should I say Greg and his secretary?' His voice fairly dripped derision. 'I happen to know Hamil's secretary. She's married with two children.'

'So you decided Greg must be buying me a love-nest. How imaginative of you.'

'It didn't take much imagination to work out what was going on. Do you deny that he bought you a new wardrobe of designer clothes as well?'

'They weren't for me. They were for his sister. I only helped to choose them.'

His mouth twisted. 'Fine, except that Hamil doesn't have a sister. And I doubt he was getting you to choose them for Sandra.'

Disgust churned inside Linden. Had Greg exploited her naïveté so callously? Pride forbade her admitting the possibility to Steed. 'What did you do, have us followed?' she asked bitterly.

'Something of the sort, with good reason as it turned out.'

'For all the good it did you,' she snapped. 'If Greg is so notorious, why is Sandra marrying him?'

His jaw tightened. 'As you're well aware, he has more than his share of charm. I've warned Sandy what she's probably letting herself in for but she's a grown woman and entitled to make her own mistakes. My aim was to ensure they weren't potentially fatal ones. Unfortunately, like many women, she's convinced marriage will change Hamil for the better.'

Linden noted the cynicism colouring his remark. It was quite obvious that nothing as benign as marriage would be allowed to change *him*. Dynamite would be more effective. 'I gather you don't hold out much hope,' she concluded.

'No, I don't, but Sandy can marry whom she chooses and I won't allow you or anyone else to interfere.'

She unsnapped her seatbelt. 'You've made your point. We're here now so you can drop me off at the entrance.'

Instead he drove in, ignoring the 'residents only' signs as he would ignore anything which got in his way, she thought mutinously. 'I'll see you to your door.'

'There's no need. It's broad daylight and I'm a big girl.'

Her sarcasm was also ignored. She had the slight satisfaction of scrambling out of the passenger door before he could come around to open it for her, marching ahead of him into the building. She was conscious of his measured tread close behind her as she reached the door and fumbled for the key. It was taken from her fingers and thrust into the lock, then he held the door wide for her to precede him.

'Would you like to come in?' she asked with deliberate irony since it was obvious that nothing she could do would make him go away until he was good and ready.

'Coffee would be good, thanks,' he said although she hadn't offered. 'While you make it I'll ring the airport and arrange your flight back to Perth.'

In the act of reaching for the coffee-maker she froze, her eyes widening with astonishment at his presumption. Anger rose in her like a cloud, fuelled by the mocking glint she recognised in his eyes. Her own sparkled with indignation. 'Am I to be tarred and feathered before you throw me out of town?'

Her anger rolled off him. 'It's a thought,' he murmured, apparently giving it serious consideration. 'I'm not sure about tar in those sun-kissed curls of yours, but feather—now *that* would be interesting.'

It took every ounce of her will-power not to heave the coffee canister at him. He was the most infuriating man she had ever met. What on earth had possessed her to cross verbal swords with him? In their short acquaintance she was already well aware of who would win.

A long, shuddering breath restored some semblance of inner calm. 'Well, you can forget it. I have no plans to leave town yet.'

He folded his arms, his expression thunderous. 'Then make them. Now you know that Greg Hamil is engaged, there's no reason for you to remain in Derby.'

The one thing he still had to learn about Linden Taylor was her stubbornness. Forbidding her to do something was like an open invitation. Also, she had her own reasons for wanting to stay and they were none of Steed's business.

'I've decided I'd like to do some sightseeing,' she said flatly, well aware of the muscles working in his jaw, a barometer to his rising annoyance with her.

'See what sights in particular?' he demanded. His crossed arms strained his white shirt across well-developed muscles. She swallowed hard, preferring not to face the evidence of how physically prepossessing he was. The experience of his kiss was proof enough.

Her throat dried as the memory forced itself into her mind. 'How do I know?' she said defiantly. 'I'm sure there's a lot to see around here.'

He inclined his head in agreement but there was no softening in the tawny gaze. 'There is, but a party girl like you wouldn't be interested in the Pigeon Heritage Trail or the marshes surrounding the town. Somehow I can't see you cheering on the sidelines of a mud football match.'

The coffee-pot almost slid from her hands. 'Now just a minute! You have no right to judge me on the basis of some cloak-and-dagger observations which can be interpreted in more than one way— and not only your way,' she added recklessly. 'Or hadn't you heard about there being two sides to every story?'

His eyes gleamed coldly. 'You're overlooking the most compelling evidence: the way you came on to me at the party.'

Her head jerked up. 'I came on to you? I wasn't the one forcing myself on my partner. I hated being kissed by you.'

His strong features reflected cynical amusement, making her itch to slap the smugness off his face. But she had shocked herself once already with such a reaction. She vowed to remain in control of herself no matter how much he provoked her, which he had no compunction about doing. 'There was no real force and no hatred at all,' he contradicted. 'You enjoyed every minute of it so it's a waste of time denying what your body already showed me.'

Damn him, he couldn't be right; she refused to allow the possibility. 'It must be a terrible burden, always having to be right,' she taunted. 'But you're wrong this time. You're also wrong about my leaving. As you observed, I've rented the flat for a month and I intend to stay with or without your approval.'

One eyebrow tilted ironically. 'I suppose you thought a month would be long enough to snare your quarry.'

Presumably he meant Greg. 'This was planned as a holiday, a chance for me to get away. You make it sound as if I came here on a...a man-hunt.'

'When nothing was further from your mind.' His silky tone emphasised his scepticism.

'Oh, for goodness' sake, think what you like.' It was bound to be the worst, so what was the point of denying anything?

He surprised her by moving to the door. 'Forget the coffee. I shan't stay.'

Had she managed to convince him of her innocence against all the odds? His capitulation seemed suspiciously sudden but she didn't want to tempt fate by questioning his decisions. All she wanted was for him to go. 'As you like,' she said with studied nonchalance. 'Thank you for the lift.'

'My pleasure.' He made it sound as if it was anything but. 'I'll be in touch.'

'Don't both . . .' But he was gone as swiftly and silently as a crocodile deserting a riverbank. The silence of the room closed around her with stunning abruptness. She watched the door anxiously, half expecting him to return. He had given in much too easily. Of course, he had said he would be in touch.

The coffee was ready so she poured herself a cup and carried it to the balcony from which she could watch the fishermen reeling in cod, salmon and catfish from the muddy waters of King Sound. The day before she had seen a young woman bring in an enormous mud crab, the flailing claws larger than its captor's hands.

She was not, repeat not, watching Steed leave, she assured herself. Despite his promise to return she never wanted to see him again. How dared he assume that she was trawling for a wealthy husband with no more conscience than those fishermen had towards their catches?

Whether Steed believed her or not, Greg *had* given her the impression that he cared about her. Maybe she had been impulsive in following him to Derby without a clear invitation but that was her only crime.

If anything, Greg had been the fisherman, using intimate dinners and armloads of flowers as bait. It was clear now what his intention had been. Far from offering her the safe haven of his love, he'd been the wolf to her Red Riding Hood. All the better to eat her.

Drawing her knees up, she rested her arms on them and lowered her head until the lively wharf was no longer in her line of sight. Her eyes burned but she refused to allow the tears to come.

She wouldn't think about Greg's being engaged. He wasn't worth her tears any more than Andrew had been. Damn, she hadn't wanted to think about Andrew either. But since it was a day for disappointments, Andrew naturally sprang to mind.

Andrew Edmett had been the boy next door in Perth. His invitations had flattered her until she'd realised that he was totally unreliable. He'd found her lack of family amusing, saying they were two of a kind since he never saw his parents. But they weren't alike. Having no roots had made Linden long for them passionately. Andrew's 'live for today' philosophy had alarmed her and his unwillingness to see his family had disturbed her.

Everything had come to a head when she'd tried to plan a Christmas break. 'Who knows how we'll feel by then?' He'd shrugged off her concern. She'd already known how she would feel—just as unsettled as she did then.

Greg had seemed totally different. A man of substance with family ties strong enough to be documented in *Who's Who*. After Andrew, she'd been a sitting duck for his brand of charm and apparent rock-steadiness. Nothing he'd said or done had suggested that he was already committed to another woman back home.

Subconsciously, however, Linden must have suspected a problem, perhaps alerted by his preference for secluded rendezvous. Why else had she balked at spending a weekend alone with him on his boat? Self-preservation was a wonderful instinct.

Too bad it hadn't come to her rescue at the first sight of Steven Dare. Pretending to be his escort at the party now seemed reckless, as out of character as following Greg to Derby uninvited.

If not for Mrs Elmira's death, Linden probably wouldn't have acted so impulsively.

The woman had been more like a grandmother than a patient to Linden. Hand-knitting, home-made preserves and the time and inclination really to talk were all qualities she associated with a real grandmother, and she had enjoyed them all with Mrs Elmira.

Linden had never wanted to help anyone as much as she did this patient. It was so cruel that her failing heart had claimed her life before Linden could make a difference. Foolish though it was, she still felt guilty.

Her boss had insisted on Linden's taking some leave. As a therapist, she needed to replenish her own resources in order to help others, she'd been reminded. She had never taken a proper holiday, either while studying to qualify as a psychologist, or later, working as a sleep therapist. The idea had suddenly been appealing.

Greg's abrupt return to Derby had decided her. She would follow him and find out what had gone wrong between them.

Well, now she knew. How Steven Dare must be laughing at her. Perhaps returning to Perth would be best.

Why give him the satisfaction? The thought flared through her mind. The Kimberley coast was still out there. Why shouldn't she explore it while she was here, as a sort of consolation prize? Steven Dare had no right to order her to leave and she didn't have to go.

Picturing his face when he found out she was still in town gave her a meagre sense of victory, displacing a little of the day's disillusionment. As a foster child, she had been shunted here and there to suit other people's whims, but she didn't have to endure it now.

Being in Steed's arms was ample reminder of her adult state if she needed it. In fact she had never felt more conscious of her femininity, or of his male power.

She closed her eyes, refusing to think of how he had made her feel, or the way his kiss had set the blood singing in her veins. Enough, she commanded herself dizzily. She reached for a folder of tour brochures which came with the flat, deliberately focusing on them to avoid thinking about him.

Her strategy was only partially successful. He still managed to disturb her dreams that night but by morning she had convinced herself that their paths need never cross again. He was hardly likely to have the same interests as a tourist in the region.

So it came as a shock to hear purposeful footsteps matching her own as she approached the tourist office next day. 'It's too much to assume you're about to book a flight back where you came from?'

Her mouth went dry and her tongue darted across her lips in a nervous gesture which she regretted as soon as she saw a responsive gleam in his hazel eyes. 'No, I'm not. It's still a free country, isn't it?'

His brilliant gaze impaled her. 'Nothing in this life is free. Everything has a price.'

'What is your price?' she demanded. He had fallen into step with her, his shoulder brushing hers.

The day was already hot but his nearness forced her internal temperature up by several degrees.

Wheeling around, he grasped her shoulders as if tempted to shake her, before releasing her abruptly. 'Nothing you'd be prepared to pay,' he bit off.

They were outside the tourist office and she stumbled through the door, shaken by her own tumultuous reaction to his touch. What if he hadn't let her go? What if...?

'Yes, may I help you?'

She reined in her runaway feelings and approached the counter. 'I...I'd like to book a tour, please.' Her voice held a betraying tremor which infuriated her. The man had barely touched her, for goodness' sake. She tried again. 'There's an overnight cruise to Winjana Island...'

'Oh, but it isn't——'

'Isn't run as often as it used to be.'

The woman looked startled then smiled as Steed appeared at Linden's elbow. 'Tomorrow's is the last for some time, isn't it, Helen?' he addressed the woman directly.

'Er...I can check.' She sounded flustered but began to push her hair back in a preening gesture which irritated Linden. Did the man have this effect on every female he spoke to?

Ignoring him outwardly while every nerve-ending registered his presence wasn't easy but Linden managed it, blessing her professional training. 'Can I make a booking now?'

She was aware of Steed and the woman, Helen, exchanging glances over her head. Perhaps Helen was an old flame, or a current one, she thought, caught off-guard as a savage sensation churned through her.

'Yes, of course.' The woman bustled with receipt books and tickets, taking Linden's details and cheque. The transaction seemed interminable, since Steed insisted on supervising. Why was he being so helpful all of a sudden?

'Was there something you wanted from me?' she asked when tension finally overcame her.

His expression made her shiver. 'You've just given me what I wanted.'

Because she was leaving town on the cruise? The thought struck like a cold shower. 'I have every intention of returning to Derby after the cruise,' she informed him tautly, 'so I wouldn't celebrate my departure just yet.'

She was aware of Helen regarding her curiously as she was handed a ticket. 'Enjoy your cruise.'

Knowing it was what Steed wanted her to do had taken some of the pleasure out of it. With a murmur of thanks Linden accepted the document. Luckily Helen engaged Steed in conversation so he was unable to follow her out of the office.

Arriving at the wharf next morning, she was glad that she had decided not to let Steed ruin the experience for her. The Buccaneer Archipelago was a maze of tiny islands, mostly uninhabited, which dotted the turquoise waters to the north of Derby. Exploring them promised to be romantic and exciting.

After some deliberation she had brought along the notes for a book she was writing about her work as a sleep therapist. Greg had shown an interest in publishing it, although she doubted whether his offer still stood. But that didn't mean she couldn't work on it while she had the time and perhaps find another publisher when she returned home.

A gleaming white cruiser rode at anchor near the end of the kilometre-and-a-half-long wooden jetty. A grizzled old seaman worked on board and looked up as she came near. 'You for the cruise?'

'That's right. You must be the Captain Bill I read about in the brochure.' She held out her ticket and he barely glanced at it before taking her overnight bag and stowing it on board. Then he held out a hand to help her.

She looked around excitedly. 'How many passengers are there?'

He jerked his head towards a door leading below. 'You're the last to come aboard. If you get comfortable I'll cast off now.'

So they were leaving right away. She settled herself on a padded banquette facing the water and watched with interest as the captain did complicated things with coils of rope. A gap yawned between the vessel and the wharf and the man straightened to wave them off.

'Aren't you coming?' she called out in alarm.

'No, he isn't. It's just you and me.'

Shock jolted through her as she spun around to meet Steed's hard features. She ran to the side but the wharf was already lost in white foam. 'No, you can't do this.'

His gaze mocked her. 'Do what? Take you on a cruise for which you've booked and paid?'

'Not with you. That's what Helen tried to tell me, wasn't it? The cruise is no longer running. So why did you let me think it was?'

'Because I wanted you where I can keep an eye on you. Captain Bill kindly agreed to play along for one day, to help me surprise a lady friend.'

Panic invaded her and she toyed fleetingly with the idea of swimming back to the wharf. As if reading her thoughts, Steed stepped between her and the railing.

'You can't keep me here. Who in hell do you think you are?'

Lashing out at him, she landed a kick on his shins but her soft pumps made no impact. All she did was throw herself off balance on the undulating deck. There was nowhere to slide except into Steed's waiting arms, which closed around her.

A suffocating sense of awareness overtook her, making breathing a challenge. She fought the sensation, to say heatedly, 'This is kidnapping. You won't get away with it!'

His wry glance took in the vast amount of ocean already between them and the shore. 'It looks as if I already have.'

CHAPTER THREE

TURNING back to the bridge, Steed resumed the controls, his movements so deliberate that Linden wanted to scream. But there was no one to heed her display of frustration other than the gulls wheeling overhead and the occasional dolphin leaping in the boat's frothy wake as they planed across King Sound.

She moved closer to Steed so that the wind wouldn't snatch her words away. 'I demand that you take me back to the wharf immediately.'

His mild glance flickered over her. 'You're in no position to demand anything. Besides, old Bill saw you come aboard of your own free will. Who's going to believe a ridiculous tale about kidnapping?'

The cold certainty that he was right invaded her. What on earth had she got herself into? 'You still haven't told me where we're going,' she tried again. Perhaps there would be some escape from him when they reached their destination.

His mouth hardened into a grim line. 'Don't pretend you don't know where Bill's tour would have taken you.'

Her grip on the railing tightened. 'Somewhere called Winjana Island for an overnight stay, then further along the Buccaneer Archipelago. Does it matter?'

'Perhaps not to you, but it would to Sandra if she found out.'

'Sandra? But I don't——'

With a savage gesture he cut the engine and silence surrounded them. The boat began to wallow and she almost lost her footing as Steed lunged towards her, saving her from falling with a brutal hold on her upper arms. 'You really expect me to believe that you don't know who owns the lion's share of Winjana Island?'

She tried to shake off his punishing grip, all too aware of the hard wall of his chest pressing her against a bulkhead. His mouth loomed disturbingly close and for an insane moment she wondered if he was going to kiss her again. Instead he gave her a little shake. 'Well?'

'No, I don't. But no doubt you're about to enlighten me.'

'With pleasure, although it can hardly be a surprise, since you couldn't wait to get there. Most of the island is owned by Greg Hamil.'

Her shock at his pronouncement must have shown on her face because she caught the briefest flickering of doubt in Steed's dark eyes. Well, let him wonder. She hadn't known the island belonged to the Hamil family or she would never have chosen to visit it. But she didn't expect him to believe her, so what was the use of denying it? 'It's included in a tour so they must welcome visitors,' she said as calmly as she could.

He shook his head. 'Not any more. Those tours were discontinued when Bill decided to retire. We only allowed them to go on as a favour to old Bill, or they'd have been stopped long before this.'

Her eyebrows lifted. ' "We"? I thought you said Winjana belonged to Greg.'

'Not all of it. What he doesn't own, I do. I hate to disappoint you but Hamil hardly sets foot on the place any more. I run the island now.'

A nightmarish sense of unreality overtook Linden. She dragged in a steadying breath. 'But surely there are other people on the island?'

'Other people who work for me.'

He was making it clear that she couldn't expect help from anyone on Winjana as long as their livelihood depended on his goodwill. And he had made sure that witnesses knew she had gone to the island voluntarily, so who would believe she was being held there against her will? 'How long do you plan on keeping me there?' she demanded with as much aplomb as she could manage. Inside she was quivering with apprehension. She told herself it wasn't at the prospect of sharing his island with him but because of his high-handed treatment.

'Until the wedding.'

Some of her poise deserted her. 'Wedding?'

Grim humour lightened his chiselled features. 'Greg and Sandra's,' he supplied.

'I thought you meant——'

'My marriage bed?' He interrupted her, a husky note in his voice which did extraordinary things to her nervous system. 'Are you suggesting it as an alternative?'

She brought her head up, meeting his amused look with cold disdain which disguised the tumult she felt. 'An alternative to being boiled in oil, maybe.'

His index finger grazed her chinline, sending shivers scudding along her spine. 'There are ways I could change your mind.'

Her throat dried and she turned her head aside to avoid meeting his challenging gaze. 'Is this the only way you can get a woman to your bed—by kidnapping her?' she asked with deliberate coolness.

'Not at all. I much prefer subtler methods, like this.'

As he drew her into his arms she opened her mouth to protest but no sound emerged. She tried to hold herself rigid in his encircling arms but the heat of his body pressing against her defeated her, turning her limbs molten. When he clasped her chin and brought her lips into line with his, she was powerless to stop the surge of emotional awareness from leaping through her. Yet she didn't want him to kiss her. She didn't want...

The force of his passion seared through her like a fireball, burning out every trace of resistance she tried to summon. Her hands fluttered against his chest and somehow found their way around his shoulders, her nails digging into his unyielding flesh as he plundered her mouth with a skill which left her breathless.

Closing her eyes against the torrent of impressions flooding her consciousness, she fought for some semblance of control. But it was like trying to hold back the tide with her bare hands. He could not have chosen a better way to humiliate her than by forcing such a response from her.

When he finally released her she was shaking. Her mouth felt swollen and she knew her eyes were slumbrous with the desire he had ignited in her. 'I hate you,' she seethed, resisting the urge to cover her face with both hands.

His eyes gleamed. 'You have a unique way of showing hatred. I could get to like it.'

She forced a tremulous smile. 'Then maybe I should try charm instead.' Right now she was prepared to try almost anything to escape from him, although she didn't feel up to examining her motives too closely.

He shook his head. 'I prefer the response you already gave me.'

'Damn you.' She looked around for something to throw at him but he had returned to the controls and restarted the engine, leaving her fuming in impotent fury. In spite of herself she became vibrantly conscious of every fluid movement, every caressing touch of his hands on the controls. Worst of all, her fevered imagination insisted on translating them into his touch over her skin. She shivered, furious with herself for letting him provoke her so. Yet there didn't seem to be any way to prevent it.

Relief coursed through her when she caught sight of an island rising out of the turquoise water. In spite of herself, her curiosity was aroused. White sand rimmed a green interior like a necklace. She caught a glimpse of buildings nestled in the greenery and a jetty angled out into the deeper water. Steed made for this and they were soon tied up, the boat rocking gently against the silvered timbers.

Steed lifted some boxes on to the jetty—supplies, she assumed—then tossed her overnight bag on to the pile before reaching for her hand. When his fingers closed around hers, she schooled herself not to react. Despite his dire warning that everyone on the island obeyed him, she was sure she could get someone to help her return to the mainland. Perhaps there would be a phone she could use to call for a boat to pick her up. If it took her entire holiday budget, she would pay whatever was asked, anything to put an end to this outrageous farce.

To still her thoughts she asked the first thing which came into her head. 'You say you own part of the island. How did you come by it?'

'I won it in a poker game.'

He couldn't expect her to believe such nonsense. 'No, seriously. Was it a family property?'

His mouth twisted into a sneer. 'My family barely owned their souls. My father was a gold prospector and my mother followed him everywhere, dragging me along. I was in my teens when they finally inherited Dad's parents' house in Derby and settled down. That was when Sandra came to live with us. We had a few years of playing happy families and then my parents' car was washed off a causeway in a flash-flood.'

Genuine compassion coursed through Linden. 'I'm so sorry.'

'Spare me.'

'No, really. I was in foster care myself when I was little, so I know what it's like not to have proper roots.'

He made a choking sound of derision. 'If you're trying to win my sympathy, save your breath. Your parents are Lee and David Taylor of Fremantle. I checked up on you after I got back from the party.'

'You did what? You bastard, you have no scruples about people's privacy, do you?'

'It doesn't pay me,' he said without a trace of remorse.

'Well, if you dug deeper you'd find they were the foster parents who took me out of a group home when I was thirteen. They gave me an education and a future. I took their name out of gratitude for all they did for me.'

There was no sign of an apology, which shouldn't surprise her by now. 'What happened to your real parents?'

He couldn't possibly be interested but she felt moved to tell him, if only to allay his suspicions about her. 'My mother had health problems and couldn't look after me so I was put into care when I was six.' She repeated the simple details passed on to her when she was old enough to ask. 'I didn't know my father.'

'Did you ever try to find your mother?'

'Of course I did, but she died years ago. The Taylors are my family now.'

'Rough deal. No wonder you found Greg so appealing.'

It wasn't true. The Taylors had been the most loving parents any child could wish for and she couldn't care for them more if she'd been their natural child. 'You never give up, do you?'

His throaty laugh reminded her of a tiger's growl. 'Something you should bear in mind.' Hefting the boxes and her bag, he led the way through the bush, leaving her no choice but to follow him to a contemporary version of an old colonial house. Orientated towards the beachfront and the striking view, it had a roofed veranda facing west. Louvres were used instead of windows to admit the sea breezes and the shiplap boards were painted white to repel the sun. An outside covered staircase led from the main building to a separate area underneath the elevated house. Above it, bifold doors opened up the front wall to the view. It would be like living in a tree house. 'You won this in a poker game?' she asked in disbelief.

'Close enough. Two of us were bidding at auction and reached a stalemate. We played cards for the right to put in the final bid.'

'The other bidder was Greg Hamil,' she guessed from his tone.

'It's the only freehold on the island his family doesn't own.'

'In that case he must have been put out when you won.'

Steed's look was scathing. 'I might have known where your sympathy would lie, but it's misplaced. Whatever you think, the land is in safer hands with me.'

Sympathy was the last thing Linden felt. After his treatment of her she was almost pleased to see Greg lose out for once, but it was hard to imagine anything being safer with Steed. 'Where are the other houses?' she asked.

He indicated a path leading through the bush. 'The Hamil compound is at the other end of Crescent Beach, but don't get your hopes up. There's no one there at the moment.'

'Surely there's someone else here?' She couldn't keep the alarm out of her voice.

'The caretakers, Chloe and Ernest, and their boy, Terry, have a place between here and the Hamils'.'

She searched out the roofline of the other house in the direction he indicated. With relief she spotted it among a stand of eucalyptus, silky grevilleas and wild passion-fruit. At least she wasn't alone with Steed. The idea of being marooned on an island with him set her pulses leaping, and not with the anger she would be justified in feeling. No, there was something beyond anger which managed to excite and repel her at the same time.

Sexual chemistry, she decided hastily. Steven Dare was a hard, worldly-wise man who had no doubt recognised the awareness which had flared between them from their first meeting and wasn't above exploiting it to his own ends.

The insolence of his kiss demonstrated his readiness to use any means he could to separate her from Greg for his cousin's sake. What would she do if he chose to use even more potent means of persuasion?

He would find that the kitten had claws, she vowed fiercely. Like Greg, he wouldn't be allowed to have everything his own way. His hijacking her to his island might keep her away from Greg but she wasn't about to be driven into Steed's arms for consolation, if that was what he expected.

Her thoughts were scattered when a small boy of about eight rocketed out of the house waving a large sheet of paper. His nut-brown skin glistened from the heat and his dark eyes shone with excitement. His features were faintly oriental and intriguing.

He held out the sheet of paper for Steed's inspection. 'I'm nearly finished. What do you think?'

Was this the caretaker's little boy? 'Are you Terry?' she asked, fascinated by the rapport between man and boy as Steed gravely inspected what she now saw was a school project sheet.

The child snorted with derision. 'Terry's a bardi, an aboriginal,' he pronounced scornfully as if she should have known. 'I'm Jason Dare.'

Dare? Startled, she looked from the child to Steed and finally saw the resemblance. 'This is your son?'

'Jason, this is Linden Taylor. She's going to be staying with us for a while.'

'Hello,' he said, suddenly shy.

'Pleased to meet you, Jason,' she responded mechanically, in the grip of an unreasoning anger. How dared Steed criticise her after acting like a bachelor when he had a wife and son at home? Hot anger swept through her at the thought of herself in his arms. No wonder he understood Greg so well. Talk about taking one to know one.

A savage unnamed emotion tore through her at the sight of Steed ruffling his son's hair, so like his own in colour. At his father's urging, the child took Linden's bag and carried it into the house.

She jerked her arm away as Steed tried to take it. 'Leave me alone. You're a fine one to criticise Greg's behaviour.'

A frown etched a deep furrow in his forehead. 'What the hell do you mean?'

'I mean you have one set of rules for others and another for yourself. Or did you conveniently forget about a wife and family when you were kissing me and pretending we were lovers at the party?'

His expression became arctic, his eyes spearing her with chilling intensity until she felt a shiver pass along her spine. He looked as if he wanted to kill her. 'For your information, my wife died two years ago in a boating tragedy.'

Her hand flew to her mouth. 'I'm so sorry; I never thought...'

'Obviously not. It's easier to judge everyone by your own dubious standards.'

She *had* been judging him but only because he was so determined to judge her. Still, she was appalled at her own behaviour. He had a way of bringing out the worst in her at every turn. This would have to stop. 'I made a mistake about you. Isn't it possible you could have done the same about me?'

His gaze was assessing, the dark eyes half hooded so that she was unable to read his reaction. 'Time will tell, won't it?'

At the steps leading up to the house, she stopped. 'I don't see how. I won't be here long enough.'

He crossed his arms over his broad chest. 'And just how do you plan to get back to the mainland—swim?'

'I'll ask the caretaker to ferry me across,' she said on a rising note of desperation.

'You may well ask.'

But he worked for Steed so there was no way he would take her side against his employer's, she thought despairingly. Her only chance was to wait until she could find a telephone and try to enlist a boatman who wasn't on Steed's payroll. Recalling how the woman in the tourist office had colluded with Steed to bring about her present predicament, she didn't hold out much hope.

'You can't make me stay,' she insisted.

His unblinking gaze held no remorse. 'I didn't make you come here and I'm not making you stay. I'm just refusing to take you back.'

'Which amounts to the same thing,' she retorted. 'You said I'd be here until Greg's wedding but there's no telling how long that will be.'

'If my dear cousin has anything to do with it, the wedding will take place sooner rather than later. So you may as well resign yourself to having a holiday right here.'

'A prison by any other name,' she murmured. There had to be a way to outwit him and she intended to find it. But for now she might as well put a graceful face on the inevitable defeat and try to have the best time she could on the island. Its unspoiled charm was already starting to beguile her although she would never admit it to Steed. 'It looks as if I have no choice.'

He looked as if the outcome had never been in doubt. 'Quite right. You can use Sandy's old room. She keeps a good supply of clothes and female bits and pieces here and I doubt if she'll need them for the present. I can replace them next time I'm in town.'

'When will that be?' She tried to sound uninterested.

He wasn't fooled. 'Long after you're gone, so don't even think about it.'

'Foolish of me,' she admitted waspishly. 'I should know by now that you get your kicks out of bullying people.'

'Not at all. I have far more satisfying ways of getting my kicks.'

A wave of warmth washed over her as he loomed closer, his mouth tantalisingly near. Kissing her was becoming a habit of his which disturbed her for all sorts of wrong reasons. But this time he merely lifted a hand and brushed her lips with his parted fingers, eliciting an audible gasp. The light touch was if anything more sensuous than the most passionate of kisses.

She swallowed the moan which gathered in her throat. Damn him, she would not give him an inch. She was staying under protest. She didn't have to like it or his high-handed manner.

'Have you any idea how much I hate you?' she asked in a voice barely above a whisper.

He shrugged. 'My shoulders are broad. Having you hate me is safer than having you love Sandra's fiancé.'

'Dad, are you coming for lunch?' a reedy voice called from inside the house.

Steed's warning glance went from the house to her. 'This is between you and me. Involve Jason and I promise you'll regret it.'

He must really have a low opinion of her to think that she would involve an innocent child in their private war. 'I do have some scruples,' she said, colouring hotly.

His eyes gleamed a challenge. 'I suppose there's a first time for everything.'

She was still seething when they went inside. To cool her temper she paid close attention to the house, noting the coolness of the limed brush-box floors, vaulted ceilings and free-flowing spaces which were clearly architect-designed.

Telegraph poles sandpapered to a glassy smoothness gave solidity to the structure and tied the roof to concrete piers set in the ground, no doubt as security against the cyclones to which the region was prone.

There were vivid decorative touches such as a Mexican quilt stretched over a frame on one wall and aboriginal paintings signed by a famous regional artist. The effect was tropical yet stylish. The handiwork of Steed's late wife? He didn't look as if he would welcome the question, especially in front of Jason.

'Chloe left us sandwiches,' the child said, indicating a tray of tempting savoury treats. He dragged up a canvas director's chair for her alongside his own and she sat down, letting Steed pile her plate with food. She wasn't particularly hungry but welcomed the distraction.

'Are you on holiday?' Jason asked around a mouthful of sandwich.

Her malevolent glance moved to Steven. 'It appears that I am. Maybe you'll show me around the island after lunch?'

'Jason has to finish his homework for School of the Air,' Steed cut in. 'He shares his lessons with Terry Shaw at Chloe's place. I'll show you around.'

Her hopes of getting to a phone died abruptly. 'Don't put yourself out. I can look around on my own. You must have work to do, or something,' she finished feebly.

'It'll get done. I'm between books at the moment and planning a new expedition. I'd hate you to lose your way.'

Or go anywhere he didn't sanction, she thought, in a temper. 'On second thoughts, I'd rather take it easy this afternoon. I'm sure there'll be time to look over the island later.'

'Suit yourself. There's a paperback library on the veranda if you want something to read.'

'Do you have any of Houdini's books?' she couldn't resist asking.

Was that amusement playing around his eyes and mouth? She could hardly believe her feeble jest had breached the wall surrounding his gentler emotions. 'No, but *The Man in the Iron Mask* or *The Count of Monte Cristo* might suit your mood,' he suggested.

In the end she chose one of his own books, *Kimberley Calling*, as much to find out what made him tick as to learn about the area. It was the story of his solo expedition by kayak from the mouth of the Prince Regent River along a dangerous stretch of coastline to the mouth of the Ord River. As she read of his encounters with sharks and man-eating crocodiles, her blood chilled. She could hardly believe that he had lived to tell the tale.

Was he the bravest man alive or the most reckless? His wife must have been alive then because the book was dedicated to Mia and Jason. What must it have been like for her, waiting at home while the man she loved was in such danger?

So absorbed was she that she didn't hear Steed join her on the veranda. 'Good book?'

Startled, she slammed the pages shut, mentally superimposing on his strong features the piratical beard he'd worn in the book. The effect was nothing short of alarming. 'I'd call it irresponsible rather than good,' she said, not wanting to admit how disturbing she found the thought of him in extreme danger.

'It's my living,' he said shortly.

'An odd choice of occupation for one who objected to being carted around the countryside as a boy,' she thrust at him.

Cool disapproval was her response. 'As it happens, the travel wasn't the problem so much as the lack of roots and security, both of which you note I have provided for my family. Not,' he added acidly, 'that it's any of your affair.'

'I'm merely returning the favour, since you involved yourself in my life,' she snapped back. Apparently the privilege was not to be mutual.

Not that she cared what he did for a living or why, she told herself. All the same it was surprisingly difficult to take the satisfaction she expected from imagining him in the jaws of a crocodile.

The atmosphere remained tense as she joined them for a meal of barramundi poached in a garlic sauce and served with rice and salad. Evidently Steed was used to cooking his own meals, despite having lunch provided by Chloe, whom Linden had yet to meet.

Afterwards father and son cleared the table and washed the dishes between them. It appeared to be a well-established routine and Linden was annoyed when it made her feel superfluous. There was no objection when she announced that she was going to bed.

Her room was spacious, cooled by a slowly rotating overhead fan. A woven cotton spread covered the vast bed, which was festooned in mosquito netting. Refreshed by a shower in the well-equipped *en-suite* bathroom, Linden was happy to arrange the netting around her and give herself up to sleep. It had been a long, emotionally draining day.

Still she was too tired and overwrought to sleep. Her thoughts drifted from Steed's book to the woman who had waited for him at home. What had Mia Dare been like? Had Steed loved her very much?

Why it should matter to her she wasn't sure. She told herself she was only trying to understand the man, the better to outwit him. Although what hope she had of defeating a man who wrestled crocodiles for a living she didn't know.

She was hardly aware of drifting off to sleep to the friendly squeals of fruit bats outside her window, until she was startled into wakefulness by a series of terrified screams. Cobwebs barred her way as she tried to struggle out of bed, until she realised it was the mosquito netting surrounding her. The screams continued as she fought free of the mesh and slid her feet into her pumps. Sandra's kimono dressing-gown lay across the foot of the bed and she thrust her arms into it. Whatever was wrong, it was coming from Jason's bedroom.

CHAPTER FOUR

'IT's coming to get me. It's coming!'

Jason's frightened voice reached Linden as she hurried down the corridor. His room was next to Steed's, she remembered. They were in a separate wing of the house from the guest wing, and now she cursed the few steps it took her to reach the child's room. Steed was already there when she pushed the door open. He had also been woken from a deep sleep, judging by his tousled hair and the shadows circling his eyes. He wore only the bottom half of a pair of pyjamas and she was instantly aware of the broad expanse of muscular chest and the curve of his hips revealed by the low-slung pants.

It was an effort to marshal her thoughts and take in what was going on. Jason lay on the bed, his eyes open and staring in stark terror. Automatically, Linden followed his line of sight but could see nothing on the wall or ceiling to explain his fear. Then he began to thrash from side to side, moaning. Steed tried to restrain him but his efforts only made Jason more agitated.

'He's awake but he doesn't recognise me,' Steed bit out as she moved closer.

Never had she been more thankful for the excellent training she'd received at the sleep centre. 'That's because he isn't awake,' she explained. 'He's somewhere between the two stages. He doesn't even know you're here.'

'Then he's having a bad dream?'

She shook her head. 'Children behave differently when they have nightmares. If it were a bad dream, you'd be able to waken him and he'd cling to you for comfort and reassurance. The best thing you can do is leave him completely alone.'

He looked furious. 'In this condition?' His sceptical tone told her that he thought she was crazy.

'I know what I'm doing. My work is in sleep therapy,' she retorted furiously. 'I work at a sleep centre in Perth where we see cases of night terrors like Jason's all the time.'

He didn't answer but she noticed that he stopped trying to restrain Jason. 'You can stay in the room to make sure he doesn't hurt himself but the more you try to restrain him, the more prolonged you're likely to make the episode,' she added.

Her heart turned over as Steed made an obvious effort not to intervene. It was hard, she was only too well aware, but it was the best course of action. The tension in him was almost palpable as he watched Jason thrash around on the bed.

Then, unexpectedly, Steed reached for her hand. The contact almost made her pull back. His skin felt fiery and his bunched muscles betrayed the effort of holding back from his son. The grip on her hand was crushing but she didn't protest. All her concern was for Jason.

'How long does this go on?' he asked in a low tone.

'They're usually over quite quickly. Look.'

Almost as she spoke, Jason's thrashing stopped. He stretched and yawned, his eyes fluttering half-open. 'Dad?'

At an encouraging nod from her, Steed took the boy's hand. 'It's OK, son, I'm here.'

Jason smiled sleepily. 'Linden too?'

Steed's expression tightened but he drew Linden into the boy's line of sight. 'Yes, son, she's here with you too.'

Jason sighed. 'Good. I like her. She smells like a mother.'

Linden's stomach clenched with compassion for the child who associated her femaleness with his lost mother. No wonder he suffered night terrors, with so much tragedy in his young life. It was so unfair.

In minutes Jason was asleep again. Steed rose and slid the covers over his son then urged Linden out of the room, closing the door gently behind them. He looked so thunderous that she wondered if he resented her interference, but she'd only tried to help. Whatever was between them had nothing to do with the little boy. 'I'll go back to bed now,' she volunteered.

'Stay,' he growled. 'I'll get us some brandy.'

It was more like an order than an invitation and her resentment flared instantly. 'I don't drink brandy, thanks very much.'

'What, then? Milk? Iced water?'

What she really wanted was to return to her own room where her senses wouldn't be assaulted by the sight of him half clad and dishevelled from bed. It was having a thoroughly disturbing effect on her equilibrium.

Moments later he returned carrying a glass of chilled water and a half filled brandy glass for himself. As he passed her the drink their hands brushed and she recoiled as if stung, spilling some of the contents on to the polished floor.

'Leave it, it's only water,' he insisted as she looked around for something with which to mop up the spill. 'Come and sit here.'

'Here' was a two-seater cane couch and he was already occupying one half. She perched uncomfortably on the other end, putting as much distance between them as she could while she sipped the water.

'Relax, for goodness' sake. You were calm enough in there, when I would have expected hysterics.'

But Linden was accustomed to dealing with episodes like Jason's night terror. It was her job. This was altogether different. She had no training or experience to equip her for a midnight discussion with a half-dressed man whose glistening torso was only inches from her own.

It was all too easy to remember the hardness of those muscles when he held her against him. The brandy beading his lips brought his kiss back with such force that she began to tremble.

His fingers skimmed her arm. 'You aren't cold, are you?'

It was a balmy tropical night and the temperature had nothing to do with her reaction. She shook her head. 'I'm edgy from being woken so suddenly.' As a lie it was close enough to the truth to be credible.

'What happened in there?' he asked.

Relief swept through her. It was easier to talk about Jason than to analyse her own confused feelings right now. 'He had what's called a night terror. Children sleep in different cycles from adults. They can wake briefly enough to frighten themselves before their conscious mind registers that there's nothing to fear.'

He swirled the brandy around the glass, the amber liquid reflecting the warm hazel of his eyes as he regarded her thoughtfully. 'In the morning I'll ask him what was the matter.'

'I don't recommend it,' she contradicted him.

He shot her a furious glance. 'Since when did you become his doctor?'

She clenched her hands tightly together, reminding herself that he was reacting as a concerned parent. All the same she felt his censure like a lash. 'It's my job. I know what I'm talking about.'

The lines in his face became less austere, his cold gaze thawing slightly. She wasn't sure whether the change was a good thing or not. It was easier not to be aware of him as a man when he was tearing strips off her.

'If something's bothering Jason, surely I should find out what it is?' he said.

She shook her head, her hair falling in a tumble of blonde curls around her face. 'He won't remember the episode in the morning. If you question him about it, you could distress him. He'll be frightened and confused if he thinks he's doing things at night that he doesn't recall in the morning.'

'Sounds like some women I know,' he shot back.

If it weren't for his alarm over Jason they wouldn't be having this conversation, she reminded herself. But it was difficult not to take it personally. 'I wouldn't know, I've never been in such a position,' she denied, annoyed to hear a betraying tremor in her voice. She didn't want him to see the effect he was having on her ragged nerves.

'Have you never done anything by night that you'd rather not recall in the morning?' he persisted.

This was getting altogether too personal for her liking. She drew the kimono tighter around herself. The gown felt uncomfortably skimpy.

'It's hardly your concern, is it?' she retorted, wishing she could think of something more scathing. 'I should think with Jason you'd have more to worry about than how I spend my nights.'

Her diversionary tactic worked for the moment, but only because he allowed it, she suspected. 'Do you think there's more to this episode than a bad night?' he asked.

'It depends whether or not it's part of a pattern.'

He rested his forearms on his knees with the glass balanced between them, like a flesh-and-blood image of *The Thinker*. 'He had nightmares after his mother died but they haven't recurred for over eighteen months, until this week.'

Compassion lanced through Linden, prompting her to ask, 'What happened?'

'While I was away on an expedition, Mia and a friend went out in the cruiser. The inboard engine caught fire and the vessel exploded. They were anchored off Crescent Beach and Jason was playing on the shore. He saw the whole thing.'

His voice was matter-of-fact but she noted that his hands around his glass were less than steady.

Evidently two years hadn't cushioned the memory of the tragedy for him.

'How terrible,' she murmured. 'No wonder Jason has nightmares about it.' She thought for a moment, and decided that the question had to be asked. 'Would you have known about them all if you're away so much?'

She had braced herself for his anger but its vehemence made her tremble. 'For your information, I haven't been away since Mia died, so yes, I'd be aware of them.'

She felt the colour sliding from her face. 'I'm sorry. I didn't mean...'

'That I was a bad parent? Of course you did. It would never occur to you that I put my son's welfare above all else in my life.'

Even his own happiness? It would explain the lack of a woman in his life. 'I never doubted it,' she said quietly. 'Jason is warm, loving and thoroughly appealing.'

His eyebrows lifted. 'Unlike his father?'

'I'd hardly be the best judge, given my position here,' she retorted.

'Quite. And yet, in spite of everything, my son seems to have taken to you.'

She hadn't missed the yearning in Jason's voice when he'd asked for her. She was surprised to feel an answering tug whenever she thought of the vulnerable little boy. 'I take it you disapprove,' she observed.

He passed a hand across his chin, which was dark with stubble, making him look even more dauntingly masculine than usual. 'If your presence helps my son, I can hardly disapprove. But don't go getting ideas that we can't get along without you. Jason may benefit from a woman's attention but I certainly don't need a wife.'

'Or I a husband,' she snapped back, infuriated beyond belief. After her experience with Greg, she'd had enough of men from this part of the world to last her for some time. 'But since you plan to keep me here at your pleasure, I'd like to use my training to find out what's bothering Jason and try to help him through it.'

'You can do that and keep your emotions out of it?'

'Objectivity is part of my training,' she reminded him.

'It didn't stop you getting involved with Greg Hamil.'

'That was different. We met at a fund-raiser for the sleep centre where I work.'

'My point exactly. You didn't separate your personal and professional roles then. Why should I trust you now?'

'All right, I did get involved with Greg through my work, but it isn't a crime.'

'Perhaps not, but it was unwise.'

'Like coming to Derby without knowing whether or not Greg would welcome my presence.'

The glance he shot her was icy with disdain. 'You're getting the idea. You do have a tendency to act first and think later.'

She could hardly deny that it was becoming a habit. She'd done it again by letting Steed escort her to the party without knowing anything about him. She was certainly paying the price now. 'I'm doing my penance by being kept here against my will,' she flashed angrily. 'Isn't it enough for you without lecturing me as well?'

She had trouble meeting his cynical look.

'You'll know when I'm satisfied you've paid for your misdeeds, although you must agree it's hardly an arduous punishment. You have the run of my house, a deserted beach at your doorstep and my personal services—as your guide,' he added in response to her involuntary gasp of protest.

She could feel the colour surging up her neck and into her face. Damn him. He was suggesting that this hateful situation should be enjoyable because he was sharing it with her. He knew exactly the effect he was having with this line of discussion. Yet he'd made it quite clear that he wasn't looking for a wife. So what did he want from her?

Remembering his insulting first impression of her, she felt her anger rise. Did he think her so fickle that she would consider replacing Greg with him? Yes, she would, a traitorous inner voice insisted. The way she felt around Steed had nothing to do with Greg. It was much more powerful, the recognition of elemental needs and desires she hadn't known she possessed until she met Steed. He had called her reckless but he didn't know the half of it. With Greg she had never felt impelled to abandon herself to the cravings of her body and give him all that he desired of her and more, yet with Steed it was a shocking temptation.

Except that he didn't desire her beyond simple sex, she recognised. To him, seducing her would be an efficient means of keeping her out of harm's way. Any pleasure he—or she—happened to derive from it would be considered fortuitous.

'What would you have done if I hadn't decided to book the cruise?' she asked on a sudden thought.

He shrugged, his massive shoulders moving with sleek grace so that she was forced to swallow hard. 'I would have found some other means of getting you here.'

She decided to test her theory. 'You mean by pretending interest in me yourself?'

His languid look roved over her, tracing every taut line in her tense pose. Still without moving a muscle, he followed the curve of her neck where the kimono had slid slightly off her shoulders, exposing the gleam of her breasts above the soft folds.

In spite of her resolve Linden felt her nipples straining against the cloth. 'I wouldn't have to pretend,' he denied, his voice a persuasive murmur. 'It would be what you might call a labour of love. Are you suggesting it as a viable proposition?'

By his own admission, he was prepared to seduce her to protect his saintly cousin. The thought gave her the strength to say, 'You flatter yourself that I'd be interested in a man who holds me captive the way you're doing.'

His throaty laughter mocked her. 'Oh, Linden, you don't fool me for an instant. When I held you in my arms, you didn't act as if you were being tortured. All I have to do is look at you and beads of perspiration break out across that alabaster forehead of yours. Even now your whole body is a quivering mass of need. Why don't you let me satisfy it? Afterwards I guarantee that leaving the island would be the last thing on your mind.'

She didn't doubt it, and the worst of it was that she was madly, deeply tempted in a way she'd never felt before. Every instinct told her that he would be a virtuoso lover, capable of demanding and giving pleasure beyond her wildest imaginings. Her reaction to his touch and his kiss proved his ability to arouse her almost beyond endurance. As a lover he would take her breath away. If only his last words didn't make his purpose abundantly clear. 'No,' she said shakily, sounding far less certain than she would have wished. 'It isn't what I want at all.'

His lashes dropped, hooding his derisive expression. 'Liar,' he taunted softly. 'It is what you want, and sooner or later you'll be forced to admit it.'

Her head turned in vehement denial. 'Never, unless you do the forcing.'

'You'd like me to, wouldn't you? Then the blame would be all mine. You could enjoy every minute of it and call it rape afterwards. Uh-uh, lady. When it happens it will be decidedly mutual, I promise you.'

'When it happens'? He sounded so sure of her that she faltered. 'I'll never admit to wanting you. There are much bigger fish in the sea.'

'Such as Greg Hamil?'

The note of condemnation in his voice shook her. She hadn't meant to suggest any such thing, only to put him down. Now it was too late to retract. 'Think what you like,' she said with a defiant toss of her head.

A cold, hard glare was his response. 'You don't know when to give up, do you?'

'Not until I'm off this island and away from you,' she vowed.

'Thanks for the warning. I'll make sure I'm a most attentive host from now on.' It sounded more like a threat than a promise.

She'd had all she could take of this exchange. The tension throbbing between them had drained her and she realised it was almost dawn. 'It's late. I'd like to go back to bed,' she said in a defeated voice.

'My sentiments exactly,' he drawled.

'Alone,' she added desperately. 'As I intend to remain for as long as I'm forced to stay here.'

Did he recognise her words as bravado? He must have done because his laughter taunted her. 'Don't forget which road is paved with good intentions.'

How could she forget when she would have him to guide her there? She bit back the retort, trying to salvage what was left of her pride. 'Goodnight, Steven,' she said with quiet determination. She could feel his eyes on her as she returned to her room with undignified haste and slammed the door between them.

She awoke to a gently rocking bed and the sight of Jason Dare bouncing cautiously up and down on the end of it. 'Good morning,' she said sleepily. He looked none the worse for his nocturnal adventure but she felt as if she had barely closed her eyes.

'It's nine o'clock,' he told her as she groped for the bedside clock. 'Dad said I wasn't to wake you until you woke up by yourself. You did, didn't you?'

'I suppose so.' She didn't want to get the child into trouble with his father.

'I've brought you breakfast.' He pushed forward a tray containing rapidly cooling toast and coffee the colour and consistency of mud.

She reached for the orange juice instead. 'Do you always give your guests breakfast in bed?'

'No. They're mostly boring business people or members of Dad's film crew. They're always cranky in the morning,' he supplied with the air of one sharing a confidence.

She laughed, liking Jason immensely. 'You'd be cranky too if you had to start work at dawn.'

'I suppose.' It seemed to be his favourite expression.

She drank some juice and nibbled on a piece of toast since he was eagerly awaiting her verdict. 'This is good.'

He regarded her compliment as stating the obvious. 'Of course. I'm a good cook.' There was a long pause then he said in a barely audible voice, 'I'm glad you came to my room last night.'

'Your dad was there too,' she contributed, surprised that Jason himself had broached the subject. As she had told his father, she hadn't intended to raise the issue for fear of alarming the child further. But now he had brought it up she decided to make the most of it.

He twisted the bedclothes into a rope, not looking at her. 'I know, but it isn't the same.'

She held her breath. 'The same as what?'

'You know. The same as having a mum. If I had a bad dream then, she could make it go away.'

'Are you having bad dreams now, Jason?'

'Not a dream exactly, but I get real scared and don't know what I'm scared of.' He gave her a shy look from beneath lowered lashes. 'Guess I'm a real baby, huh?'

She shook her head, her heart going out to him. 'Everybody gets scared sometimes, even grown-ups. Maybe I can help you find out what you're scared of and together we can make it go away. What do you think?'

He shrugged offhandedly but there was a suspicious brightness in his eyes. 'If you want to.'

'I do want to. Thanks for letting me help.'

'Would you like to see the island after your shower?' he asked as she pushed the covers back. The change of subject wasn't lost on her.

'Yes, I would,' she agreed, touched by his eagerness for her companionship. His need for a mother figure was heart-wrenching. 'Don't you have school today?' she asked.

'Course not. Today's Saturday.'

'So it is.' She'd lost track of time since arriving in Derby. 'In that case, I'd be honoured to have you show me your island.'

He giggled. 'It isn't really mine but I pretend it is sometimes. How did you know?'

'Because I used to pretend too. When I was your age, I lived in a big old house with lots of other children who didn't have families. There were two grown-ups to look after us. I used to pretend they were my parents and the big house belonged to just my family.'

His eyes widened. 'Then you didn't have a mother either?'

'Nor a daddy. I'll bet you're glad to have a daddy who cares about you?'

'It depends,' growled a voice from the door and they both jumped. How long had Steed been standing there?

'On whether I'm in trouble or not,' Jason guessed, suppressing a giggle.

'I thought I told you not to disturb Linden.'

She hastened to the child's defence. 'He isn't disturbing me. He's going to show me around.'

Steed nodded. 'Good idea. We'll all go together.'

He was only making good his vow to keep a close eye on her, she realised. 'There's no need. I'd hate to keep you from your work.'

'As Jason pointed out, it's Saturday. We could all use a rest day.'

It was unlikely to be restful given the charged atmosphere between them which was as oppressive as the air before a thunderstorm. How long before it broke? She wished she hadn't promised Jason her company, then she could avoid Steed too. But she couldn't disappoint the child who hovered beside her like an eager puppy. 'I can be ready in half an hour,' she agreed.

'Fifteen minutes or we come and get you,' Steed asserted, to Jason's obvious delight. When she didn't argue he shooed the child ahead of him out of the room.

Showering took five of the fifteen minutes and deciding what to wear another five. For someone who used the island only rarely, Sandra kept a good wardrobe here. Using the other woman's things was a forcible reminder of why Linden was here, dampening her pleasure at the beauty of the outback morning.

Jason was waiting impatiently when she emerged wearing a long-sleeved shirt in a reptile-print cotton, teamed with high-waisted denim jeans which made her legs feel as ungainly as a colt's. Steed spared her hardly a glance as he handed her a straw sunhat. He and Jason wore the bushman's Akubra felt hats. 'Let's go,' he said.

Where the backyard ended the bush began, but the wildlife recognised no such boundaries. Jason eagerly pointed out a yellow-throated miner gathering cake crumbs from an outside table, and a blue-tongued lizard drinking from a bird-bath.

As they emerged on to a bluff overlooking the aptly named Crescent Beach, Linden drew in her breath at the magnificent vista. Indented with bays, the coastline was ringed by rock walls layered in colours from red-brown to cobalt. The surging waters were riddled with reefs where fish leaped in silver cascades and an immense turtle floated peacefully off-shore.

'It's glorious,' she said, her voice catching as she reminded herself that she wasn't here from choice.

'Hard to believe it was an iron ore mine until a few decades ago when work transferred to Cockatoo Island,' Steed observed in a gruff tone.

This explained the ageing jetty which looked much too substantial to service a holiday settlement. Around it a few small boats bobbed on the water like the tropical equivalent of a suburban car park. Linden looked back, catching sight of the Hamil property screened by a thin line of paperbarks. 'Is there no other development on the island?'

He shook his head. 'The rest is a bird and wildlife sanctuary. Greg had some ideas of developing this cove for tourism but without my parcel of land it isn't viable.'

Studying his hard profile, Linden was glad that he stood between Greg and his plans. From the little she'd seen so far, the island was much too idyllic to despoil.

'What are you thinking about?' Steed asked suddenly.

'Greg and his plans,' she replied truthfully, regretting it when his face immediately darkened.

'I should have known.'

'No, it isn't what you think.' But he was already striding down a path towards the jetty where Jason was staging a naval battle between warring factions of driftwood.

With a heavy heart she watched them as Steed joined in the battle. As he crouched beside his son, his masculine toughness was tempered by a glimpse of the boy he must have been. Wild and reckless, always off on some adventure of his own, most likely. Those qualities still existed in him and, tempered with a sharp intellect and powerfully masculine body, it was a combination to make her limbs weaken.

Unexpectedly he looked back at her and she reddened, her thoughts far too transparent on her face. 'When it happens...' His words swirled through her consciousness. She dragged her eyes away, afraid that if their eyes met again he would see what she didn't want to admit even to herself. If he kept her here much longer, his possession would become harder and harder to fight.

'No,' she said aloud, needing to hear it in her own ears. How could she hate him so much, yet want him with every fibre of her being? She had to get away before surrender became inescapable. She only hoped it wasn't already too late.

CHAPTER FIVE

'It seems a shame for only a handful of people to have all this to yourselves,' Linden observed as the tour continued, this time to the wild interior of the island where a sandy track led to a fresh-water stream and a pool ringed by pandanus palms, creepers and tall grasses. She had found it was easier to focus on why she disliked him, than to endure a confusing mixture of feelings.

Steed reacted angrily, flecks of gold sparking in his eyes. 'We don't keep it to ourselves. Bird-watchers and serious naturalists have the run of the island. I see myself as a custodian for future generations, but I don't expect you to understand.'

Oh, but I do, she wanted to assure him. But it was safer if he thought she sided with Greg on developing the cove. His disdain burned her like a brand but it kept a barrier between them for now at least.

Jason had climbed a white-limbed eucalypt and called down to them from its heights, 'There's a boat coming into the jetty.'

Her heart leapt. A new arrival meant the chance of getting a ride back to the mainland. At the same time the thought brought an unwanted feeling of distress. But it was only at the prospect of leaving Jason before she was able to help him properly, she told herself.

'It's only Ernest bringing supplies for Chloe,' Steed dismissed the news. 'We're joining them for lunch today. She doesn't get many visitors so she's anxious to meet you.' He lowered his voice. 'For Jason's sake, I expect you to behave yourself.'

'Don't worry. You've already made it clear that I can expect no help from your underlings,' she seethed.

His hand clamped around her arm. 'They may work for me but they're also my friends and I expect you to treat them accordingly. Ernest may be our caretaker but he's also a tribal elder, and Chloe is a member of the local aboriginal council, so you'll show respect. Understood?'

'Yes, master,' she murmured mutinously, her face flaming.

What a low opinion he had of her, she mused later. As if she would inflict their quarrel on such a charming couple. Chloe's softly spoken welcome disarmed Linden at once, as did their son, Terry. About Jason's age, he could have been his twin. They were obviously as close as brothers.

Chloe had prepared a delicious lunch of salad and chilled crab, caught by Ernest that morning. 'How long are you staying?' he asked during the meal.

Before Linden could answer, Steed cut in. 'Now she's seen the island, Linden can't tear herself away.'

Chloe regarded her speculatively. 'Are you sure it's only the island which has captivated you?'

Her face burned and she pretended rapt interest in her lunch. Chloe seemed pleased with the idea that Linden might be interested in more than the scenery. 'What else could there be?' she asked tensely.

'You never know what you'll find here,' Chloe said, winking at her. 'One thing my people taught me is that what you're looking for may be right in front of you. My Ernest, now, he lived across the way from me at Lombadina. Saw him every day from I was thirteen and still he had to convince me he was the man for me.'

'Didn't take much convincing,' Ernest grumbled, with a fondness which belied his gruff words.

A hot flash of jealousy speared Linden. How lucky they were to have grown up belonging to their land and to each other. It was a kind of belonging she despaired of ever knowing for herself.

She pushed her plate away. 'Thank you for the delicious meal, but I think I've had a little too much hot sun today. I'd like to go back and lie down for a while.'

She had been afraid that Steed would insist on following her back to the house but miraculously he let her go, probably to avoid arousing his friends' curiosity. It was a relief to be alone. Her thoughts had never been more turbulent and confused. Ignoring them was an effort but she focused on the need to locate a telephone. Steed must have some means of contacting the outside world. How did he deal with film crews and publishers?

Since it wasn't in any of the main rooms it had to be in Steed's study, which was under the house, accessible by an outside covered stairway. She felt like a sneak-thief as she let herself into his workroom.

The door opened on to a large open-plan room lined with shiplap boards painted white for coolness. Louvres instead of glass in the windows admitted currents of air from the ocean. She looked around with interest. This was where Steed wrote his books and planned the documentaries of his expeditions. Against a wall was a worn sofa draped in hand-woven fabric. Above it were displayed photographs of his adventures. In many of them he cut a solitary figure against the splendour of the Kimberley coast, the stubble of a beard darkening his chin. He looked leaner, harder and even more heart-stoppingly attractive.

Several family snapshots showed him with a much younger Jason and a beautiful Filipino woman who must be Mia. She was so fragile and beautiful that Linden could understand why Steed had married her. She resembled a perfectly formed china doll, her delicacy the perfect foil for his rugged masculinity.

She swallowed as a huge lump filled her throat. She had heard the revealing huskiness in his voice when he'd described losing Mia. Did he still mourn for her? Was that why he rejected any suggestion of another woman taking her place?

Not that Linden had any such notion. How could she be attracted to a man who treated her as he did? She would be a fool to give in to the kind of brief encounter he was offering, especially knowing why he was offering it. 'When it happens', he'd predicted. Well, it wasn't going to happen. She was leaving long beforehand.

Among the computer equipment, camera gear and mountains of reference books she found what she was looking for, only to stare at it in frustration. Why hadn't she realised that Steed would have a radio telephone? And she had no idea how to use it.

Dispirited, she went back upstairs, considered resting and decided her thoughts would give her no peace. Instead she changed into her bikini. Steed's pool boasted a spectacular view over the bay and neighbouring islands and she'd been dying to try it. Only his reaction to her brief bikini had restrained her. While he was otherwise occupied she could have a quick swim and change before he returned.

She gave a blissful sigh as she slid into the crystalline water and began to swim lazy laps. Ignoring her presence, yellow silvereyes darted down to drink from the pool like living flashes of sunlight. Steve was right. It was paradise.

Pulling herself out of the pool, she intended to rest for a few minutes on the tiled coping. She was almost asleep when a shadow darkened the sun. 'Hello, Linden.'

With the sun behind him she had trouble recognising the man looming over her until he crouched down and offered his hand to help her to her feet. 'Greg? Where did you come from?'

'With Ernest on the supply boat,' he explained. 'He told me you were here. We need to talk.'

Greg hadn't released her hand and his fingers tightened when she tried to pull free. 'What about? You and Sandra?'

He frowned. 'I don't blame you for being upset. I didn't mean you to find out the way you did.'

Her head twisted to one side. 'I don't think you wanted me to find out at all.'

His breath hissed between even white teeth. 'I tried to tell you in Perth but the moment never seemed right. Sandy's the girl next door. My family took it for granted that we'd marry.'

'As soon as she came into her inheritance.' Steed had told her about the money Sandra had come into when she'd turned eighteen. It was impossible to keep the bitterness out of her voice.

She shivered with reaction as his hand slid down her bare back, scattering droplets of water. 'This isn't to do with money although Dad's glad she has her own means, I suppose. Hell, you don't know what family expectations can be like.'

'No, I don't, because I don't have a family, or at least not one your parents would consider suitable.' She managed to free herself. 'All the same, Sandra's nice. I hope you'll be happy together.'

He dried his palms on the sides of his immaculately tailored drill trousers. 'You make it sound so final. What if I tell you I still care for you?'

It was the last thing she had expected him to say. 'I probably wouldn't believe you.'

He reached for her but she dodged him. 'It's true, Lin. You're beautiful and you're special. I didn't realise how special until I saw you at my party with Steed. I want us to be together.'

What was the saying about an ill wind blowing someone some good? Steed had intended to convince Greg she was his but instead had made him jealous enough to want her back. She had never suspected that he felt strongly enough about her to end his engagement. This must be what he had come to tell her.

Only days ago she would have welcomed the news. Now she felt strangely empty. 'There can't be any love without trust.'

'I know and I promise to be completely open with you in future, if you'll give us another chance.'

For a split-second she allowed herself the luxury of imagining what marriage to Greg would mean. She would have a family, a place in society, a home. How tempting those things seemed to someone who'd grown up without them. Greg must love her very much to risk his father's wrath by giving up Sandra.

'It isn't only a question of trust,' she said firmly, pushing the seductive images out of her mind. 'It takes much more to make a marriage.'

Horror winged its way across his face before he masked it. 'Did you think...? Oh, Linden. I wouldn't dream of pressuring you into marriage. I want us to have what we had before in Perth.'

She recoiled as if stung. 'You mean a sordid back-street affair, hiding from anyone who could possibly recognise you?'

Greg looked around in alarm. 'Keep your voice down, will you?'

'Why should I? Did you expect me to say, Greg, darling, what an irresistible proposal?'

He greeted this remark with a wolfish grin. 'Something of the sort. Then I'd be able to do what I've dreamed of doing ever since I saw you at my party.'

Before she could stop him he swept her into his arms, his mouth closing off her cry of protest. His hands were hot and heavy on her back as he held her rigidly against him, trying to force her unwilling lips apart to permit him entry.

Suddenly she was aware of brisk steps on the wet coping. 'I assume you're congratulating Linden.' Steed's voice cut through the steamy air like the crack of a stockwhip. Surprise made Greg release her and she stepped away, shivering in spite of the heat. How much had Steed heard and seen? His rapier glance warned that whatever it was had displeased him. Ice glinted in the look he turned on her.

'Congratulations?' The merest tremor gave away Greg's chagrin at being caught out by Steed.

'You do know we're engaged to be married?'

'Well, I... Of course you have my congratulations.'

When her knees threatened to give way with shock, Steed's arm was instantly around her, drawing her close. His gold-flecked eyes resting on her with apparent fondness felt as penetrating as laser beams. She knew exactly what was going on. Pretending they were engaged was the most expedient way to keep her away from Greg until he and Sandra were married. What would he do if she simply denied it?

Steed must know she wouldn't cause a scene for fear of hurting Jason, whom she had promised to help. The little boy had suffered enough in his young life. How could she add to his distress? The only way to avoid it seemed to be to go along with Steed's charade, at least for now. But inwardly she was simmering with anger. 'How could you tell

Greg we were engaged?' she demanded as soon as Greg had walked away.

Steed's indulgent expression was replaced by icy disdain. 'I realise it cramps your style to be known as my fiancée, but I warned you not to try to come between Sandra and Greg.'

'It was a pity you didn't warn Greg,' she snapped back, hurt that he so easily allocated all the blame to her.

'He wasn't the one who needed it,' he said coldly, 'judging by the enthusiasm with which you were greeting his proposal. "Irresistible", I think you called it.'

Had he arrived moments earlier he would have heard the whole of her response to Greg, instead of the most damning part.

What was the use of trying to explain when he was more likely to believe his own ears? 'You're determined to think the worst of me, aren't you?'

'And you're determined to demonstrate it.' His fingers gripped her shoulders as if he was tempted to shake her. 'At least, as my fiancée, there's a limit to the damage you'll be able to do.'

'Because Greg will tell Ernest and it will be all over Derby that I'm your private property,' she concluded. 'You may as well have put a brand on my forehead and been done with it.'

There was no humour in the way his eyes skimmed her curves which the tiny bikini did little to conceal. 'Believe me, I can think of much more effective ways to ensure your compliance, not all of them unpleasant.'

He moved closer, running his hands lightly down the tops of her arms. She reacted to his touch as if it were fire, its heat scorching along every nerve-ending. All the protestations she should have made died on her lips. She couldn't even think coherently, far less order him to stop.

Her legs turned to jelly as his hand slid inside her bikini-top and he began to caress her. His other hand was warm against the small of her back, moulding her against him. Her palms, which had been pressed against his shoulders, slid imperceptibly around until they linked behind the strong column of his neck.

His muscles felt rigid against her sun-warmed skin. Her softness yielded to his hardness and her senses began to swim. Unconsciously she tilted her face upwards, her lips parted in anticipation.

'When it happens'. . .

What was she doing? He had said he would do anything in his power to ensure his cousin's happiness. And that included a fake seduction to go with the fake engagement. His lovemaking had no more sincerity behind it than Greg's insulting proposal.

She began to struggle and felt herself slipping on the wet coping. She clutched at him, taking him with her as she tumbled backwards into the deep end of the pool.

Water invaded her mouth as she sank to the bottom. Moments later she was hauled to the surface and held in strong arms as Steed trod water beside her. She twisted in his grasp. 'What are you trying to do, drown me?'

His eyes blazed. 'What am *I* trying to do? You were the one who hauled me in. Is this the thanks I get for saving your life?'

'I'll show you who needs saving.' Ducking out of his reach, she struck out for the far end of the pool, the style which had won her swimming medals in her teens coming back fluently.

The water churned behind her as he took up the challenge, racing her. His clothes hampered him but their fingers touched the coping at almost the same moment. Without her head start, and properly dressed, he'd have beaten her easily.

Her chest heaved as she waited for his condemnation. Astonishingly, however, he began to laugh, the warm, mellow sound turning her limbs to jelly. 'Good grief, I haven't had a workout like that in years.'

'Me neither,' she confessed, startled to find herself enjoying the moment of rapport. What was happening here? 'I didn't mean to pull you in,' she said, hearing an infuriating huskiness creep into her voice. It had to be the exertion, surely?

His mouth eased into a smile and his eyes locked with hers, their intensity mesmerising. 'If I thought you had, I'd make sure you paid dearly.'

Weakness invaded her body at the promise implied in his threat. Unnerved, she looked away. 'You and whose army?'

'I get the feeling I wouldn't need an army to conquer you right now, Linden, would I?'

Would he? Or would she simply surrender? Mortified at the possibility, she jackknifed over his outstretched arm and came up at the steps leading out of the pool.

By the time he joined her she had dragged a towel around her trembling shoulders. She couldn't believe how strongly she had been attracted to him in the water. What had happened to change things so rapidly between them?

He hadn't shouted at her for one thing, although she had probably ruined his clothes. And he *had* tried to save her. He couldn't have known she didn't need saving. She must be confusing gratitude with something else. Hold that thought, she told herself as he walked towards her.

'Thank you for coming to my rescue.' Heavens, how prim and proper that came out, she thought.

'My pleasure.' Almost idly he began to work the towel up and down her shoulders. The feel of his fingers through the rough-textured fabric set her nerves aflame and she reared back. Annoyance with herself coloured her tone.

'I'd better get dressed.'

Her curtness drew a questioning look. 'There's no hurry—you won't catch cold here. This is the tropics, remember?'

It was difficult to remember anything when he looked at her so intently, as if committing every feature of her face and body to memory. 'I'm sorry about your clothes,' she said, reaching for the most mundane thing she could think of to defuse the tension crackling in the air between them.

'They've been through worse.'

In his photographs, some of his clothes looked as if they'd been slept in, as doubtless they had. 'I know. I saw your photos.' Too late, she clamped her mouth shut.

'You saw the photos in my office,' he supplied for her, his face darkening. 'I was wondering when you'd admit to snooping in there.'

Caught out, she felt her face flood with colour. 'I was not snooping. I was looking for a telephone.'

'To call Greg?'

'How could I? I didn't even know he was on the island. If you must know, I intended to charter a boat to take me back to the mainland.'

He tutted softly. 'Is that any way for a newly engaged woman to behave, running away from her fiancé at the first opportunity?'

She rammed her clenched fists on to her hips and faced him defiantly. 'I'm not newly engaged, am I?' She gave a slightly hysterical laugh. 'You only did it to spoil my chances of being a mistress.'

The disgust in his face appalled her. What had she said? She had never for an instant considered accepting Greg's offer. She had only said it to repay Steed for riding roughshod over her. But he looked at her as if she'd crawled out from under a rock. 'If all you want is to be a man's mistress, it can be arranged,' he said with dangerous emphasis. He moved towards her and she stood rooted to the spot, too stunned to react. This time there was no gentleness in him as he scooped her into his arms and crushed her against his chest, his hungry mouth finding hers with the accuracy of a love-seeking missile.

As she parted her lips to protest, his tongue probed deeply, setting up an answering yearning in the depths of her being. She clutched at him involuntarily, overwhelmed by the strength of her own arousal and confused by it all at the same time.

'Put me down, please,' she begged, tears threading her voice. There had been not an ounce of tenderness in his kiss and she was appalled at how easily he had evoked a response from her.

He set her back on her feet. 'Being my mistress obviously doesn't have the same appeal for you.'

She had had about all she could take. 'I have no intention of being any man's mistress. After what you've put me through I may decide to join a convent.'

He shook his head in blatant disbelief. 'You wouldn't last five minutes.'

Her head lifted as she flashed him a look of pure fury. 'You have a wonderful opinion of me, don't you?'

'You're forgetting it isn't opinion any more, but first-hand experience.'

'Only up to a point,' she spat. 'A point beyond which you will never be allowed to go.'

With a lightning gesture, his fingers gripped her chin, forcing her eyes up to his. 'Never say never.' His searching look made her quail. Had she tempted fate with her rash assertion? Abruptly he released her. 'Go and get dressed.'

'Aren't you coming?'

'I've decided to have a swim first, since I'm already soaked.'

'But your clothes . . .'

His jaw hardened. 'It's either a swim or a cold shower, unless you want me to prove your brave statement wrong right here and now.'

Realising how close she had pushed him to the limits of his control, she fled back to the house. By the time she gained the veranda his clothes lay scattered over the grass and foam surged from the pool as he ploughed relentless laps through the water.

Her own self-control was in shreds as she let herself into the house and took refuge under the needle-sharp spray in her bathroom, her own equivalent of a cold shower. Her arms should be bruised where he'd gripped her, but the only marks were invisible, mostly around the heart.

Distantly she heard Jason come in, having spent the afternoon playing with Terry. When she heard his cheerful, off-key whistle, her heart went out to him. However tempted she was to leave the island at the first opportunity, there were still his feelings to consider.

As an orphan, brought up in foster homes, she knew only too well how much it hurt when she was the one left behind, the adults in her life leaving without explanation. How could she do such a thing to Jason? He had already suffered the tragic loss of his mother. Linden felt bound to honour her promise to help him over his night terrors. No matter what she thought of Steed, she intended to keep her word to his son.

She knew exactly what her boss at the sleep centre would say—that she had lost her objectivity where Jason was concerned—and he'd be right. She saw too much of herself in the child and she didn't want to be the one to hurt him any more than he'd already been hurt.

The child was nowhere in sight when she emerged, clad in a silk caftan she'd selected from Sandra's wardrobe as a confidence-booster. Passing his room, she heard him splashing in the shower and smiled. The chance to help him was the only bright spot in this disastrous affair.

She was bustling around the well-equipped kitchen when Jason joined her. 'What are you doing?'

'Making you a special dinner. I know Chloe left a casserole ready but I thought you'd like crêpes better.'

He looked intrigued. 'What are crêpes?'

'A kind of pancake.' She was rewarded when his smile broadened. 'I saw a herb garden behind the house. How about picking me some parsley and chives to go in them?'

'Sure. Are we going to have a dinner like a real family?'

'If that's what you'd like.' She had a feeling it was the last thing that Steed would welcome but he was the one who had started it with his farce of an engagement. If she used the opportunity to get to know Jason better, and find out what was bothering him, Steed had only himself to blame.

She needn't have worried. When Jason returned bearing handfuls of aromatic herbs, he had a message for her. 'I just saw Dad in his fishing clothes, heading for the boat-house. He said we weren't to wait for him.'

She should have been relieved, but contrarily she felt cheated that Steed had gone fishing on what was, technically, their betrothal night. He was only making it clear that the engagement was to keep her away from Greg, and for no other purpose, but she found her eyes misting despite telling herself that she didn't care.

With an effort she calmed herself by focusing on Jason. He was surprisingly good company, showing a fascination with her stories of life as an orphan, probably identifying them with his own motherless state, she surmised. But his conversation gave her no clues to the cause of his nightmares.

After dinner she let him teach her his favourite computer game, which involved the player escaping from a ruined castle by using intelligence and dexterity. In spite of herself she enjoyed the challenge and saw with surprise that over an hour had gone by.

'I thought this game had a half-hour curfew?' she said with mock-severity.

Jason's look was angelic. 'Half an hour each,' he pointed out. There was no arguing with his logic.

'You're good fun, Linden,' he said when she was tucking him into bed. 'I wish you could stay for ages.'

Smoothing the sheets around him, she found herself wishing much the same, much to her astonishment. It was only because Jason needed her help, and not for any other reason, she told herself.

Steed still hadn't returned, so she got out her book notes and began to work on them. After today she had to accept that Greg probably wouldn't want to publish anything she wrote, but she still felt that perhaps she could interest another publisher.

Concentrating was difficult when every sound brought her eyes swivelling to the front door. Finally she gave up and took herself off to bed.

Lying alone, she was haunted by the feel of Steed's arms around her. It was as if he were in the bed with her, so overpowering was her awareness of his presence. His warmth radiated through her and she moistened her lips against the remembered pressure of his mouth on hers.

It needn't have ended there, she was well aware. He was quite amenable to having her as his mistress, she recalled with a hot flush of anger, some of it at herself for putting the notion into his mind.

Or had she? Belatedly she remembered his satisfaction at besting Greg in a poker game over the right to this property. Maybe he saw this as another chance to be one up on Greg. It was a chastening thought.

Well, he was about to find out that Linden Taylor had some say in this too. She wasn't the prize in some macho game between him and Greg, and she vowed to make it clear to him first thing in the morning.

CHAPTER SIX

LINDEN had reckoned without Jason's night terrors. Her eyes had barely closed when his screams roused her. Struggling into a robe, she hurried to his room.

Steed was already there, still wearing his fishing clothes. With traces of beard shadowing his jaw, he looked more like a pirate than ever. She shivered in spite of the night's warmth.

He frowned when he saw her but made no move to send her away. Because he knew Jason needed her, not because he wanted her here, of course. Still, they *were* supposedly engaged so he might acknowledge the fact, she thought, startling herself as she moved to Jason's bedside.

'The same as yesterday?' she asked, pain for the little boy shafting through her as she watched him thrash around on the bed.

'The same.' Bleakness invaded his tone and she found herself wishing fervently for some way to help. But Steed had already moved away any breakable objects. There was nothing to do but wait out the episode.

It ended as before, with Jason subsiding into normal sleep, reassured by their presence at his bedside. Afterwards, Steed took it for granted that she would join him in the living-room.

'Nothing for me, thank you,' she insisted when he offered her a drink. After the previous encounter, she didn't trust herself to accept even iced water from him.

He poured himself a Scotch and added ice. 'You didn't have to get up. Now I know what to expect, there's no sense in two of us having a disturbed night.'

'I wanted to help,' she assured him with quiet conviction. 'I care about Jason. He's a delightful little boy.' She crossed her arms defensively across her body. 'You don't believe me, do you?'

His fingers cupped his jaw. 'I believe you, even though your caring posture is at odds with the woman I saw trying to seduce another woman's fiancé by the pool.'

Tears stung her eyes but she blinked them back furiously. If she wasn't careful, he would have her doubting her own innocence next. 'I'm surprised you can stand being engaged to me even for convenience's sake.'

Annoyance shadowed his features. 'Naturally I don't expect a woman like you to understand a concept like self-sacrifice.' His slashing gesture silenced the protest she started to make. 'Fortunately your understanding is less vital than your co-operation.'

Her jaw clenched convulsively. 'You made sure I'd co-operate when you made it impossible for me to leave here.'

Bitter cynicism greeted this remark. 'It can hardly be said to have cramped your style.'

She swung away from him. 'Oh, go to hell.'

'Precisely my destination. Except that you're coming with me.'

Confusion swamped her, forcing her to turn back. 'What do you mean?'

'The Kimberley coast isn't exactly hell, but it's close enough if you don't know how to handle it. That's where we're going.'

Defiance blazed in her answering look. 'I'm not going anywhere with you.'

'Yes, you are. Unless your avowed wish to help Jason was more play-acting?'

'Of course not, but——'

'Then you're coming. Because I've worked out what's causing his night terrors.'

He wasn't making sense. 'What do Jason's night terrors have to do with the trip you're planning?'

'Everything. The last time I went away was the time his mother died.'

She was beginning to understand. 'Subconsciously he thinks that if you go away something terrible will happen, like the last time.' Unthinkingly, she grasped his arm. 'It has to be the answer. Children often have night terrors when something happens outside their control, like a house move or a major loss. If he hasn't been separated from you since your wife died, he's bound to be terrified of what may happen.'

'So I decided to take him with me to prove that nothing will happen when I go away.'

At the sleep centre she'd spent hours discussing problems like Steed's, but never before in her nightwear with the darkness closing around them like a velvet cocoon. She tried to thrust away the awareness of him which threatened to overwhelm her, but her voice came out much lower-pitched than usual. 'It's the ideal solution.'

'Good. Then we're agreed.'

'We're not agreed about anything. You can't make me go with you.'

His stony glare dropped the temperature in the room by several degrees. 'You'd rather I left you here with Hamil than took you along to help Jason?'

It was a damning indictment. 'No,' she said miserably, knowing that once again he had won.

It was insanity, committing herself to days in the wilderness with Steed, but at least she would have Jason for a chaperon. But who would chaperon her errant thoughts and a body which betrayed her every time Steed came near her?

She tensed as he closed the distance between them, his hands falling heavily on to her shoulders. 'This will be a research trip, scouting locations for a new documentary. You'll have plenty of time to work with Jason while I'm scouting locations for the film.'

Striving to shield her emotions behind a wall of professionalism, she failed miserably. Why hadn't he kept his distance? She closed her eyes as her senses were assaulted by a heady blend of sea scents and his own powerful male pheromones. It was a devastating package. 'Isn't there anyone else who could look after him?' she husked.

The derision in his voice made her cringe. 'I take it you'd rather stay here in case Hamil crooks his little finger?'

'You put paid to that by telling him we were engaged.'

'It worked.'

Anger blazed through her eyes. 'It's a wonder, when it must be obvious to anyone that we don't agree on anything.'

'Except one.' His head lowered and a lump rose in her throat, almost choking her. 'A very mutual desire.'

His closeness almost blanked out coherent thought. 'No, you're wrong,' she denied, her senses drowning. 'We can't even talk to each other.'

'I had other means of communication in mind,' he drawled.

Cupping the back of her neck, he squeezed gently and a sigh of pleasure escaped her, despite her best efforts to contain it. His fingers contracted and released in a persuasive massaging motion which left her feeling limp.

The temptation to lean into his embrace and allow his strong arms to enfold her was so powerful that it was all she could do to withhold a groan of assent. Yet to do so would be to admit that he was right, she did desire him. She was damned if she'd give him the satisfaction. It wasn't as if it was true, after all.

All the same, a sensation like hunger gnawed at her as she lowered her eyes to meet the sensuous curve of his lips. She'd never known a touch as compelling as his. It made her feel like a piece of potter's clay, his for the moulding into whatever shape he desired.

His hand slid down her back, bringing her closer, and she gave a faint gasp as she realised that the response was far from one-sided. The physical evidence was plain.

'Shocked?' he queried when she tensed. 'I've made no secret of the fact that I want you.'

'Nor of your reasons,' she said with a nonchalance she was far from feeling. She was well aware that he only wanted her because Greg was interested in her.

His hand dropped and he moved away until he was silhouetted against the window with the ocean outlined in phosphorescence behind him. 'So you prefer Hamil's romantic conniving to honest desire? You disappoint me.'

Shakily she gathered her wits. 'Well, I'd hate to spoil a perfect record.'

His stern gaze transfixed her. 'I'll live. But understand this. I won't have you disappointing Jason over this trip. We'll need to stock up on supplies in Derby and I want your word you'll behave if I take you back with me.'

Being on the receiving end of too many broken promises as a child made her well aware of the heartache it caused. There was no way she intended to disappoint Jason. 'You have my word,' she conceded, privately promising herself that it was all she intended to give him.

Jason's reaction was reward enough when Steed broke the news to him at breakfast next morning. 'You mean it? I can really come with you? Far out.'

Steed nodded. 'I said so, didn't I? You can help with the reconnaissance for my next film.'

'What's a recon . . . recon . . . ?'

'Reconnaissance. It means we're taking a look to see what's out there.'

Jason frowned. 'But you already know what's out there.'

'Linden doesn't.'

She waited tensely to see how he would take the news. His grin broadened. 'Linden's coming too? Oh, wow. This will be the coolest trip ever.' Then suspicion clouded his features. 'You're not coming to babysit me, are you?'

She returned his glare with wide-eyed innocence. 'You're much too big for a babysitter. I hope you'll show me some of the countryside while your dad's busy working.'

He spooned cereal with renewed enthusiasm. 'No problem. Course I haven't seen too much myself yet, but I do know what a crocodile slide looks like. I could show you one.'

'As long as you remember everything I've taught you about safety in crocodile country,' Steed intervened. 'It's up to you to keep Lin safe, understand?'

She shot Steed a surprised look. He actually sounded as if her well-being mattered to him. 'It's a big job for a small boy,' she told Jason.

He drew himself up. 'I'm not small. I can wrestle them crocs if you need me to.'

Her eyes met Steed's and she saw him struggling not to smile. In Jason she had a momentary glimpse of Steed at the same age, every bit as eager to take on the world's challenges. The arrogance of the male species, she thought wryly. Yet it was also the key to their undeniable charm. At least to one man's charm, the thought sprang to mind, catching her off-guard.

They *were* a charming pair, she was forced to admit as she surveyed them serenely, like a matriarch admiring her family while acknowledging their flaws. The thought made her chest tighten painfully. Her family. Was this how it felt to be part of a real family?

They almost made a nuclear family, she saw. One more child to fill the empty seat across the table. Steed's child. A girl, her fanciful thoughts insisted on supplying.

'She isn't listening, Dad. Look, she's gone all dreamy-eyed.'

Linden came back to them with a rush. 'I was no such thing.'

Jason hooted derisively. 'Yes, you were. Liar, liar, pants on fire.'

'Enough, Jason,' Steed reproved, but there was laughter in his voice. 'Wherever you were, it made you smile. Care to share it with us?'

What would he say if she obliged? Luckily Jason filled the breach. 'She was imagining being saved from a man-eating crocodile by a brave hunter—who looked just like you, Dad.'

Steed's eyes gleamed speculatively. 'Is that so?'

'Of course.' Her relieved laughter joined with theirs. 'And the hunter had a terribly brave son who gave the alarm.'

'That was me,' Jason contributed.

Soon they were all laughing and embroidering the outlandish tale until the real reason for her reverie was submerged in an unexpected glow of good feeling.

At last Steed stood up. 'I'd better start planning the gear for the three of us.' He ruffled Jason's hair, his mood mellower than she had yet seen it. 'I suppose you can't wait to tell Terry your news.'

'You bet.'

Linden's smile followed the child as he rocketed out of the door. 'This trip is the best medicine anyone could have prescribed.'

'And not only for Jason,' he agreed in such a soft voice that her head came up, her eyes startled. 'It seems to agree with you too.'

Awareness of how much she'd allowed her guard to slip during the breakfast made her sharpen her voice. 'I'm merely putting a good face on things for Jason's sake.'

'Of course you are.'

He didn't sound convinced. What on earth had he glimpsed in her face while she'd been lost in foolish daydreams? 'Don't get the idea I'm looking forward to this trip,' she snapped, very much afraid that he already suspected the truth.

She did want to go, and not only because of Jason. Yet it made no sense. She couldn't be softening towards Steed with all that stood between them, could she?

Mechanically she stood up and reached for the plates. 'I'd better make myself useful by cleaning up in here.'

His sharp look raked her. 'You can leave it for Chloe if you prefer. Suit yourself.'

In small matters but not anything important, she noted angrily. 'Jason told me that Chloe has Sundays off and their family goes to afternoon church on one of the neighbouring islands. I'm sure she'd rather not come back to a whole day's chores tomorrow.'

A V of annoyance creased his forehead. 'It isn't like you to be so thoughtful. You wouldn't want to be left alone for any reason, would you?'

'Such as going off for a clandestine meeting with Greg? I could hardly do it with you working below, could I?' In truth, the idea hadn't occurred to her until he'd suggested it. 'As it happens, I have some writing I can do,' she said wearily.

His eyebrows arched. 'Love letters, Linden?'

'Pleas for rescue. I intend to put one in a bottle and toss it into the sea.'

His amused look stayed with her as he went outside. His footsteps sounded heavy on the staircase leading to his workroom. She pictured him settling down at his computer watched by the photographs of his past expeditions, and a disturbing thought came to her. Was he angry over her offer to do the housework because he resented seeing her taking the place of his late wife?

'I certainly don't need a wife,' he had assured her the last time she had inadvertently trespassed on this territory. It was a wonder that he could stand even a mock-engagement if it was such a sensitive issue. It was a measure of how important Sandra's happiness was to him.

Moodily she immersed the dishes in clouds of soapsuds, her hands barely moving. What must it be like to be totally loved by Steed, so that he rejected even the thought of another woman in his life? she wondered. She was unlikely ever to find out.

Her eyes were misty as she finished the dishes. It was only when she heard the roar of an outboard engine that she realised Greg was leaving by boat. Another victory for Steed.

She was glad that she had packed the notes for her book. Working on them kept her mind occupied until Jason returned, announcing that Terry and his family had left for church. She consoled him by playing the computer game with him for a short time, then enticed him to the pool for a swim.

By the time Steed rejoined them for lunch she had almost convinced herself that concentrating on Jason could defuse the impact of his father on her quivering senses.

Almost.

The first test came next morning when Steed announced that she was to accompany him to Derby to organise the needed supplies. 'Can I come?' Jason appealed, his eyes liquid.

Steed shook his head. 'Sorry, son. It's a school morning. You'll be coming with us soon enough.'

Linden wished he could come with them now but it wasn't fair to use the child as a buffer because she couldn't stand on her own two feet. He needed his schooling and she needed to assure herself that every encounter with Steed didn't turn into another seduction scene, at least in her mind. He would probably laugh if he knew the effect he was having on her. More points for him to score against Greg Hamil. It was a mental reminder to keep her defences up.

All the same her eyes kept drifting to him as he steered his powerful cruiser over the foaming waves of King Sound and in to anchor at Derby. He had opted to use the vessel as the easiest means of transporting the supplies back to the island.

'Why does the town need such a long wharf?' she asked as they tied up.

'Derby has the second highest tidal range in the world—eleven metres,' he informed her. Gesturing at the coffee-coloured waters around them, he added, 'At low tide all this becomes mud-flats, swarming with skipper fish.'

'I saw it from my flat, acres and acres of ochre-coloured mud glistening in the sun. I meant to take before and after pictures so the people in Perth will believe the tides are so huge.'

He offered her his hand to help her out of the boat. 'Do you miss the city?'

'I miss the Taylors and the people I work with but not the city itself,' she said after a moment's thought. 'The light here is so bright it almost hurts the eyes. I thought it would be all golden sands and bluer than blue water but it's quite different, isn't it?'

'*Café au lait* water and mud-flats. You must be disappointed.' The censure in his voice grated on her.

'I'm not in the least disappointed. It's the most glorious place imaginable—so rugged and challenging.' Like some of its inhabitants, she couldn't help adding to herself. 'I could live here quite readily.'

'If your plans had worked out,' he concluded tersely.

He meant if she'd been engaged to marry Greg, she thought with a flash of annoyance. To him she was neatly pigeon-holed under G for gold-digger. She shouldn't care what he thought, but somehow the realisation stung.

She was frustrated with herself for reacting when his opinion shouldn't matter in the least. 'You should be pleased that my "plans", as you call them, didn't work out. If they had I wouldn't be accompanying you on your expedition, would I?'

His jaw hardened. 'Thanks for the timely reminder.'

She could have kicked herself. Despite knowing the rivalry which existed between him and Greg, she had suggested that the trip came second to being with Greg, when nothing could be further from the truth. It could only increase his interest in possessing her. An unwanted frisson of excitement chased along her spine. Surely she didn't want to encourage a competition, with herself as the prize?

Of course not. Greg had killed any affection she might have felt for him with his insulting invitation to become his mistress. So why did she persist in goading Steed with her unavailability?

He had accused her of wanting him to force himself upon her so that the blame would be all his. Could it be true? She resolved to guard her comments more carefully from now on. Maybe Jason wasn't the only one with a hidden psychological agenda.

Steed dropped her at her rented apartment while he organised the supplies. 'Aren't you going to stay and supervise my packing?' she asked in mock-disbelief.

'Should I?' he drawled, leaning against the doorframe.

'No.' Her defeated reply acknowledged that she had given her word. 'I'll finish up here and meet you at the Chinese Gardens in Clarendon Street in time for lunch.'

He nodded tautly. 'I wouldn't advise you to be late.'

She could well imagine his response if she tried it. All the same, she welcomed the chance to shop for essential cosmetics, sunscreen oil and the like which would be needed on the expedition. It would also be pleasant to have her own clothes again, attractive though Sandra's wardrobe had been. But perversely she felt cheated of Steed's company as he drove away.

It seemed like an age since she had left the flat, although in fact it was less than a week. It made no sense but she'd felt more of a sense of belonging on the island in borrowed finery than she did in the rented flat with her possessions around her.

The mail was meagre: a letter from the Taylor family giving their news, and a note signed by everyone at the sleep centre which made her smile. It reversed the usual holiday greeting with the message, 'You're having a wonderful time, wish we were there.' If only they knew how complicated her life had become since she'd left them. Far from being the relaxing adventure she'd envisaged, the trip had confused her more than ever.

There was one more letter. Greg Hamil's return address was printed on it. Had he written to ask her forgiveness for being so presumptuous, or was it a repeat of his insolent proposal? She didn't really want to know right now. There was too much to be done before she met Steed again.

The flurry which went through her at the thought of him was alarming. Greg's letter aroused no such response. Surely it should be the other way around?

Tossing the unopened letter on to the dining-table, she set about packing for the expedition. Most of her clothes were still in her suitcase so it was only a matter of adding her personal needs and the chore was done. She left the case near the front door where Steed could collect it after lunch.

Clarendon Street was quiet as shoppers avoided the heat of the day. Linden began to wish she'd done the same. By the time she'd chosen postcards to send to the Taylors and her workmates, written innocuous messages on them and dropped them into the postbox, she felt totally enervated. Desperate for a cool drink, she chose the first café to hand and slumped into a seat in the blissful cool of the air-conditioned interior.

'Linden, how nice to see you. Mind if I join you for a second?'

Laden with parcels, Sandra Cochran slipped into a seat opposite her. Green eyes sparkled like emeralds under her fiery red hair. 'Congratulations.'

The heat had dulled her senses momentarily. 'Hello, Sandra. Why am I being congratulated?'

'Your engagement, of course.' The other woman lifted her left hand from the table. 'Steed hasn't even had time to buy the ring yet. Is that why you're in town today?'

At Linden's stricken look, Sandra squeezed her hand then released it. 'Uh-oh, it's supposed to be a secret, isn't it? Trust me to open mouth and insert foot.'

Her crestfallen look increased Linden's sense of panic. 'It's all right,' she tried to reassure Sandra. 'You're Steed's family. I suppose it's still too new to take in.'

'Haven't quite digested it yet?' Sandra twisted the solitaire diamond ring on her own engagement finger. 'I know the feeling. It's like a dream. Not everyone approves of Greg—especially Steed—but I know he's right for me.'

Thinking of Greg's letter waiting for her at the flat, Linden hoped that Sandra was right. 'The main thing is it's what you two want. No one else's opinion matters,' she said firmly.

Sandra beamed. 'Thanks. I knew we were going to be friends when we met at Greg's party, but I never dreamed we'd end up almost sisters.'

Guilt tormented Linden. Steed's rash announcement of their engagement might have deterred Greg but it was bound to end up hurting Sandra. And what about Jason?

A waitress took her order for iced tea but Sandra declined to join her. 'I'm meeting friends for lunch. Don't worry, I won't say anything about your news till you're ready to announce it properly. But I'm thrilled for you both. Don't hate me for saying this but I never thought Steed would take the plunge again.'

'You mean because of Mia?'

'He thought the sun rose and set around her. They met when he was making a film in the Philippines. They fell in love and married in a whirlwind courtship.' Her face fell. 'I shouldn't rattle on about her. You're the one who's important to Steed now. You have my very best wishes.'

She left after bestowing a sisterly kiss on Linden which left her feeling more fraudulent than ever. She wondered if Sandra knew how haunted Steed still was by his late wife. He reacted angrily to any suggestion of another woman taking her place. It said a lot for Sandra's importance to him that he was willing to pretend to be engaged on her account. The web was becoming too tangled for comfort.

She nursed her iced tea until it was time to meet Steed at the Chinese Gardens. She had passed the restaurant on her shopping trip so had no trouble retracing her steps.

When she asked for him she was shown to a courtyard at the rear, shaded by green netting which also served to deter flies. Lush green plants in baskets gave the courtyard a cool, tropical atmosphere. Fans swept lazily overhead.

He was already seated and stood up when she joined him. 'I hope I'm not late,' she said by way of a greeting.

'On time to the minute. I loaded the gear on to the boat then came in here to cool off.'

Being with him again felt like a reunion although she had no right to any such feeling. She hid behind a menu to compose herself and the words blurred before her eyes. She chose a dish of the delicious fresh-water prawns known as cherubim, served in a shallot and ginger sauce, and put the menu aside. 'I ran into Sandra this morning,' she informed him tensely.

'Naturally you took the opportunity to tell her about Greg's visit to the island.'

It had never crossed her mind. 'Of course not. I was too busy fielding questions about our so-called engagement.'

The success of his strategy evidently pleased him. 'At least it gave you something safe to talk about.'

Her temper reached flashpoint. 'Safe? She's already planning the wedding.'

'Weddings can be unplanned,' he said blithely, turning aside to give their order to the waiter.

Wanting to hit him, she restrained herself until the waiter left. 'Doesn't it bother you to be playing with people's lives? What will you do if Jason finds out?'

Flinty colour sparked in his eyes. 'He isn't likely to find out unless you tell him—in which case we'd have to get married, wouldn't we?'

How could he speak so calmly about it? The very idea of being married to him played havoc with her emotions. 'When it happens'... That damned phrase again. She had never considered a wedding night as the *when* and it was almost her undoing. 'Go to hell,' she said with angry emphasis.

Wine had magically appeared in their glasses and he raised his in a mocking toast. 'To a hell of a honeymoon, then.'

Yet again he had twisted her words to suit himself. The prospect of spending the next few days in his company in the isolation of the Kimberley wilderness seemed even more foolhardy. But she couldn't back out for Jason's sake. She made an effort to still her internal chaos. 'Whatever you say, *darling*.'

His answer was a sardonic lift of an eyebrow. 'I may just hold you to that, *darling*.'

Somehow she got through the meal. The prawns were a local delicacy but she was too distraught to enjoy the meal. Was it too much to wish for a cyclone—just a small one—to save her from going with him?

Unfortunately the skies were clear when they returned to her flat in a taxi to pick up her luggage.

Hefting the case as if it weighed almost nothing, Steed looked around and spotted Greg's letter lying on the table. 'You missed some of your mail.'

If he saw the name of the sender he'd assume that she had encouraged Greg to write to this address and his anger would know no bounds. The thought made her quail and she snatched up the envelope. 'It's not important. I can read it later.'

Before he could react she had stuffed it into a side-pocket of her holdall. It was time to go and she wasn't nearly ready.

CHAPTER SEVEN

THE subject and title of Steed's documentary was *The Return of the Crocodile* and he particularly wanted to visit an isolated waterfall along the Prince Regent River. The journey involved threading their way by boat among the hundreds of islands which formed the Buccaneer Archipelago.

The serrated coastline added many kilometres to the journey but provided endless large and small bays to explore. If Steed expected Linden to show signs of boredom he was in for a surprise. She might be here under duress but she was determined to make the most of it.

His boat, *Dreamtime*, was a sleek twenty-metre-long white-hulled cruiser with every modern device for comfort and safety including a desalination plant to produce fresh water. Linden had her own cabin and tiny bathroom. If not for Steed's cabin being right next door, she could have convinced herself that she was a tourist on a cruise, instead of his reluctant hostage.

As it was it required a determined effort to block out the sounds of his occupancy which penetrated the thin cabin walls. It was hardest late at night when the slightest sound was magnified. She fancied she could even hear his breathing in the stillness.

At least he didn't know how he affected her, she consoled herself. Since they'd set off he had kept his distance in a way which should have pleased her, but instead left her feeling slightly neglected. It was due to Jason's presence, she felt sure, and couldn't decide whether she was glad or sorry.

For some reason she was particularly aware of him today as they left the cruiser riding at anchor in St George Basin and set off in the tender down-river towards the cascades. Even watching Steed winch the small boat down to lie against the larger boat's hull had been a turn-on. His muscles gleamed with exertion in the humid morning air.

As the blue swells of the Indian Ocean gave way to the milky inland waterway, she found her eyes straying to Steed again and again as he steered the boat, alert for ripples marking snags. He was half standing, one hand controlling the outboard motor. How much in command he looked, relaxed yet watchful, his dark eyes narrowed against the sun.

Her heart picked up speed and she looked away, concentrating on the parrots which flew in bright flashes overhead. At the hornet buzz of the motor, rock wallabies came upright, their ears erect, before bounding off from ledge to ledge.

Jason was so excited he could barely contain himself. 'Did you know a lady was eaten by a crocodile at the cascades?'

She shuddered. 'No, I didn't.' No doubt it was the reason for Steed's interest in that particular spot.

'Well, she was. You're not supposed to swim there and she did and——'

'Jason, that's enough.' Steed's sharp injunction came as he saw Linden turn white.

She gave him a shaky laugh. 'I hope the crocodile isn't still there.'

He looked grim. 'There are plenty more.'

She suppressed a shiver. It was hard to reconcile the beauty of the ochre-coloured battlements pocketed with rainforest and stilt-rooted mangroves with anything brutal or deadly. The two faces of the outback, she accepted reluctantly. Now she understood why Steed had placed his rifle in the boat before they'd left the cruiser.

About twenty kilometres along the spear-shaped gorge they came to an opening in the mangroves where a jewel-coloured waterfall dropped fifty metres from the cliffs above. Linden's breath caught at the sheer beauty of the white plumes of water tumbling down the rocks between pockets of greenery. The tide-filling pool looked inviting. 'Are you sure we can't swim here?' she asked.

Steed swore softly. 'Are you being deliberately obtuse? Look.'

Hurt by his tone, which was one he might have used to reprimand Jason, she looked where he pointed. Not half a dozen metres from the boat, a dragon-head was half submerged in the green depths. It was so close, she could clearly see the horned eyebrows, reptilian skin and gleaming yellow eyes.

Instinctively she drew closer to Steed, not daring to rock the boat. 'Don't they scare you at all?'

He gave a brittle laugh. 'Only a fool isn't scared when looking death in the face. This is their territory. We're the interlopers.'

'Is that the theme of your film?'

He nodded, his hands busy with his cameras as he recorded angles and shots which might be useful to him later. It seemed to take forever and she was thankful when it was time to ride the outgoing tide back to the cruiser.

'Why do you do it?' she asked when they were safely back on board. After a lunch of salad and freshly caught mud crab, Jason had retired to his cabin to rest. She and Steed were alone in the saloon.

He cradled a frosted can of beer. 'Do what?'

'Go looking for danger.'

He scowled as if considering telling her to mind her own business, then he linked his hands behind his head. 'I suppose because it finds you one way or another, even if you stay at home and mend fishing nets.'

'But surely it takes a little longer if you stay at home?'

He swung his feet to the floor and glared at her. 'It only feels longer.' His deep breath rasped between them. 'For years my mother believed that everything would be fine if only she had a secure home of her own. Inheriting my grandfather's house didn't prevent them from being swept off that causeway, did it?'

She recoiled from his vehemence. 'No, but...'

'Until then I had intended to become something nice and safe, like a teacher. Losing my folks showed me that real security is something you find inside, not in bricks and mortar or a nine-to-five job.'

'But what about Jason?'

'What about him?'

She spread her hands wide. 'Doesn't he need you to be there for him?'

'I am there for him in every way which matters. But this isn't about Jason, is it?' His searching look impaled her.

'I don't know what you mean.'

'Yes, you do. My lifestyle threatens you because of your own childhood, doesn't it?'

She felt a lump rise in her throat. 'Is it any wonder? Living in group homes with other orphans and paid carers doesn't exactly instil certainty. At least you had parents. Now you have a son. Yet you risk everything to satisfy some... armchair traveller.'

Bitterness etched lines across his forehead. 'It obviously hasn't occurred to you that my son is one of the reasons why I do what I do. Around us is one of the last unspoilt wilderness regions on earth. Sharing it with the world through books and films might help it to survive into my son's future.'

'I hadn't thought...' she said in a strangled whisper. His passion had triggered a response deep inside her, as if an electric current had been switched through her body. Her pulses picked up speed and she was forced to look away from the intensity glittering in his dark gaze. Dear lord, she could easily drown in their depths.

'Fortunately I don't require anyone's approval,' he went on, thankfully unaware of the turmoil raging inside her. 'Although it would be educational to know who *does* fit your image of the ideal husband and father. I suppose it would be Greg Hamil, even though fidelity isn't in his vocabulary. Or is that an added attraction?'

Her face flamed and she looked away, unable to bear the censure evident in his appraisal. 'Greg did seem...established,' she said with difficulty, unsure why she should feel moved to explain herself to Steed, especially over another man.

'Rich?' he queried lazily.

'No. I'm not a fortune-hunter, no matter what you insist on thinking. Oh, how can I make you understand?'

'That you wanted roots, a family tree, someone to be there during the long nights. I understand all right. What I don't see is how you think Hamil can measure up.'

'I don't...' She stopped. Under no more illusions where Greg was concerned, she didn't expect Steed to believe her. 'I don't owe you any explanations,' she said instead.

'Yet you expect them from me,' he said coldly. 'Very well, I'll draw my own conclusions as to how you got your claws into Greg.'

It was so unfair that a cry of protest escaped her lips. 'It wasn't like that. He asked me out.'

He waited for her to elaborate. She didn't want to talk about Greg when it was Steed himself who occupied a much larger place in her thoughts these days. But if she didn't at least try to tell her side of the story, she could well imagine what a damning picture he would paint of the courtship.

'He was interested in the work of the sleep centre,' she went on, her tone defensive. 'His family is a main benefactor and he came to a fund-raising event we held.'

'And you made sure you caught his eye.'

'As it happens I stayed well in the background. I don't normally go to such events and I felt a bit out of my depth. Greg was the one who sought me out. He was charming company and he called me for a date the next day.'

'Which you accepted, of course.'

His sarcastic assurance that she had leapt into Greg's arms and his bed at the first opportunity inflamed her to screaming-point. 'Of course,' she snapped, goaded beyond endurance. 'You're the expert on seduction. I don't have to tell you how it goes, do I?'

His tongue clucked reprovingly. 'My, my. Perhaps you should tell me. I might learn something.'

'I think you'd surpass my skills in that department,' she retorted.

'Shall we put it to the test?'

'No, thank you.' But her quickly indrawn breath gave the lie to her denial. It would be so blissfully easy to immerse herself in his embrace, and not for the purpose of any comparison between him and Greg. No, her motives were much more carnal than that.

His amused chuckle brought anger to her rescue. 'Stop it, please. If you must know, the night I met Greg I was in no mood to play the seductress because I'd just lost one of my favourite patients.'

She hadn't intended to tell him about Mrs Elmira but his quick flaring of interest urged her on. 'What happened?' he asked, leaning forward.

'I told you, she died.'

His hand slid across the table, his fingers closing around hers. 'There's a lot more to it, isn't there?'

Her eyes brimmed and she blinked hard. 'Yes. Mrs Elmira came to us with sleeping difficulties but nothing I did seemed to help her. She was old and frail and her heart gave out before I could really do anything for her.'

Through the surge of grief she was supremely aware of his fingers threading through hers although she tried to still the fluttering in her stomach. 'She was more than a patient to you, wasn't she?'

'She had become like a grandmother to me, something I'd never had before.' Her free hand pounded the table. 'I should have been able to do more for her.'

He shook his head. 'There are some things we just can't fix, despite our best efforts. You couldn't cure old age any more than I could avert the flash-flood which took my parents.'

Her voice dropped. 'But it doesn't stop us wanting to, does it?'

'No, and it doesn't stop us from blaming ourselves for being the ones left behind.' His fingers tightened around her wrist. 'That's what you're really saying, isn't it? That Mrs Elmira shouldn't have died and left you behind just the way your mother did years ago.'

His perception shook her to her core and she made a strangled sound, half-denial and half-agreement because she knew he was probably right. Why hadn't she seen the connection for herself? She was the psychologist, after all. Her injured pride protested at finding him right yet again. How could he possibly know her better than she knew herself? If this went on, she'd soon be confessing how much she was enjoying being on the expedition with him. Where would her defences be then?

She took refuge in anger. 'If the lecture's over, you can let me go now.'

He took his time releasing her, his index finger gliding over the hammering pulse at her wrist. Her insides betrayed her by turning molten even as she snatched her hand back and returned it to the safety of her lap.

'There's no need to feel badly about grieving,' he pointed out. 'I know it must be difficult to acknowledge that you're human like the rest of us, but remember I do know something about love and loss.'

Contrition swept through her as she realised that she must have unwittingly reminded him of his own loss. How could she have been so insensitive? While going on about Mrs Elmira, she hadn't given a thought to how it must remind him of his own wife's death. 'Do you think it ever stops hurting?' she whispered.

A muscle worked in his jaw before he answered. 'Life never stops hurting. It's the price we pay for being able to feel. Trade in pain and suffering and you lose the ability to feel pleasure and joy. We just have to learn to live with both extremes.'

Mia again. Linden stirred restively. Could she possibly be jealous of his allegiance to his late wife? It would have to mean that he meant something to her and she couldn't... wouldn't consider it. Apart from being totally one-sided, it was the last thing she needed. Loving and losing was bad enough, but it was worse to love someone who had no room in his life for love.

Emerging from his cabin, Jason ended the discussion by asking when they were going to set up camp on shore. Although they had slept aboard the cruiser the previous nights, Steed had promised his son at least one night ashore. Linden was torn between looking forward to the experience and fearing the dangers which lurked at the water's edge.

Finding a suitable site was the first challenge. In many places the ochre sandstone cliffs came right to the water's edge, preventing beaches from forming. Steed aimed for a pebbly crescent backed by mangrove swamps and anchored well offshore to prevent the cruiser's being beached on the mud-flats at low tide. They went in by tender and Steed scoured the area for signs of crocodiles before he allowed her and Jason to step ashore.

Camp was set up on a wide rock-ledge well out of the crocodiles' reach. The surrounding waters were so blue that it was hard to tell where the ocean met the sky but for a thin line of islands marking the horizon. At their feet bush debris and logs floated up and down with the surf, accompanied by a symphony of bird-calls. With a pang, Linden found herself wishing she were here of her own volition, instead of at Steed's instigation.

Jason was helping his father to bring the rest of their gear up from the tender so she decided to look around. A small creek opened off the beach and two giant pelicans stood guard at the mouth of it. Clear fresh water bubbled over the rocks before merging with the sea water. Pushing through the trees, she was entranced to find thousands of butterflies fluttering among the cool rock-faces.

Suddenly a shadow fell across her and she screamed as a dark hand reached for her. Hearing her, Steed came crashing through the undergrowth. 'What is it, a snake?' he demanded.

Fear struck her dumb and she pointed shakily towards the man lingering in the shadows. She shrank behind Steed as the man came forward. His skin shone like ebony and the raised whorls of initiation scarred his chest and shoulders. He held out his hand. 'G'day, mate.'

Bursting into laughter, Steed shook the man's hand and answered in an aboriginal dialect. Then he turned to her. 'This is Mudgee, an old friend from Kuri Bay.'

Feeling her face burn, Linden stepped forward. 'I'm sorry I screamed. I didn't expect to meet anyone here.'

A dazzling grin split his features. 'Specially not a head-hunting cannibal, right, Steed?'

'Too right.'

The laughter in his voice incensed her. 'Go ahead, make fun of me. I know there are no head-hunters or cannibals in Australia. You're probably a computer programmer or something.'

The man found this highly amusing. He turned to Steed, ignoring her. 'She's OK, this one. Where'd you find her?'

This was too much. 'He didn't find me. I'm a tourist, not lost property.'

Steed said something in the aboriginal dialect and Mudgee replied, grinning broadly. Sure that it concerned her, Linden could do nothing but simmer with annoyance until the male laughter abated.

Seeing her ill-concealed fury, Steed finally relented and asked in English, 'What brings you up here?'

'My boy, Mick. It was time he learned the old ways.'

'So you're teaching him.'

Mudgee nodded. 'I see you got your boy with you too.'

Jason had been hovering beside his father. 'Hello, Mudgee. Yeah, Dad decided he needed my help this time.'

At his swaggering tone, Linden concealed a smile and saw Steed do the same. She had never seen Jason look more like his father and a curious pang gripped her.

Mudgee's hand grasped Jason's shoulder. 'Why don't you come with Mick and me to hunt some bush tucker? That's if your dad can spare you.'

Jason gave Steed a beseeching look. 'Could I, Dad? Mick's my mate. I've never gone hunting with him before.'

'Why not? It'll be good for your education.'

With a whoop of triumph, Jason scampered down the beach to retrieve his personal gear. Mudgee went with him. 'You aren't serious about letting him go off into the bush, are you?' Linden asked uncertainly.

'He's in the best hands. Spending a night in the bush might allay some of his fears.'

Her eyes went wide. 'A night? But he's only eight.'

'And Mick is nine, old enough to start learning about the land. You wouldn't think twice if Mudgee were a Scout leader, would you?'

'N-no, I suppose I wouldn't.'

'So what's the difference?'

The difference was in her, she acknowledged inwardly. She hadn't reckoned on spending a night alone in the wilderness with Steed. 'It still seems wrong,' she said, avoiding his eyes.

He turned her around to face him and she met his taunting look head-on although she quailed inwardly. 'I've made my decision.. Jason is as safe with Mudgee as he would be with me—safer in fact, since this is Mudgee's dreaming place, his birthright. He knows it better than any man alive.' His relentless gaze bored into her, seeing more than she wanted him to. 'You aren't thinking about Jason's night but about your own.'

Sooty lashes veiled her response. She wasn't about to tell him that she was more concerned with her *own* behaviour than his tonight. It was getting harder and harder to recall all the reasons why she should dislike him. 'I'm not in the least worried about tonight,' she said with defiant emphasis.

He gave an impatient growl and thrust her away from him. 'Perhaps you should be.'

He forced his way past the trees curtaining the creek entrance and the branches closed around him, leaving her alone and shaking.

By the time she returned to the rock-ledge he was shouldering a backpack. He picked up his camera. 'I'll be at the top of the waterfall if you need me, well within screaming distance.'

'Don't hold your breath,' she muttered savagely. She didn't look up as he left but her ears registered every scrape of his boots on the sandstone as he climbed.

The rock-ledge was shaded so she spread out her sleeping-bag as a rug and reached into her holdall for the medical thriller she was currently reading. She'd hardly opened it since coming to the Kimberley. Too many other distractions.

With the book came an envelope. It was Greg's letter, thrust into her bag before they left Derby and still unopened. Lethargically she slid a finger-nail along the fold and took out the single sheet of monogrammed notepaper.

She began to read.

Dear Lin,
I owe you an apology for my suggestion the other day. It was way out of line and I hope it won't mean the end of our involvement. Those nights I spent with you in Perth shouldn't be wasted. Remember, this is my baby as well as yours. Call me when you're back in town.

She looked at the letter for a long time. It should cheer her that Greg still wanted to be involved in publishing her book. In line with his axiom that time was money, he wanted to profit from the nights he'd spent at the sleep clinic, observing what went on. The idea had been hers, to convince him of the usefulness of a book on sleep therapy. But he could hardly call it 'his baby' when his main contribution had been an offer to consider publishing it.

He must know that she wouldn't care to be in-volved with him any more, even in a business ca-pacity. Crumpling the letter, she thrust it back into the holdall and pulled out some underwear which needed laundering. She was too restless to read. Perhaps she could reach a decision about the book while her hands were busy.

There was a rockpool near the water's edge and she carried her laundry to it, soaping each garment carefully before plunging it into the refreshing water. Spread out on the rocks, her things would be dry before nightfall.

Without warning, a force like a runaway train lifted her bodily away from the pool and slammed her against the cliff-face behind it, winding her. Clutching the stones which bit into her soft palms, she stared in bewilderment at Steed, who stood between her and the pool, his rifle held across his taut body. His face was wild, his eyes blazing with an intensity which made him barely recognisable.

'What is it?' she forced out, too winded for comfortable speech.

He kept his eyes on the water, biting his words out over his shoulder. 'Do you have a death-wish or something? Didn't I tell you to take water back to the camp? Never, ever linger at the water's edge in crocodile country.'

Her eyes swam, blurring the dark shape that he indicated with a jerk of the rifle. It was cigar-shaped and about twelve feet long. The yellow eyes and bony ridge of nostril were barely visible above the water. She jammed a hand against her mouth. She had been only inches from death when Steed had wrenched her away.

'Oh, dear heaven,' she moaned, her blood chilling. 'I didn't see it.'

'You never see the one that kills you.'

He waited until the crocodile retreated into the deeper water before he lowered the rifle and came back to her, propping the weapon near to hand against the cliff. 'Are you all right?'

She held up her abraded palms. 'It's nothing considering what could have happened.'

Shadows as dark and dangerous as the crocodile clouded his gaze as he brushed the gravel from her hands. One after the other he brought them to his mouth and kissed the hurts away. The touch of his tongue as it curled against her palm sent goose-bumps racing down her spine. She swayed, the shock catching up with her, and he caught her to him. His arms were like steel bands around her and his curses beat at her sensitive ears. His anger was like a living thing, a firestorm of emotion breaking around her.

She buried her face against his shirt. 'Why are you so angry?' she asked.

At her muffled question he slid a hand under her chin and lifted her shocked face so that she was forced to look at him. Lines of strain radiated from his eyes and mouth. 'Don't you know?'

'I know I forgot the rules but that's no reason to teach me a whole new vocabulary,' she protested, puzzled by the husky vibrancy in his voice.

'Forgetting the rules can be fatal out here. If I hadn't looked down from the top of the waterfall and seen the croc in the water...' He left the rest mercifully unspoken.

A shiver rippled through her as she noticed the state of his clothes. They were shredded where he'd hurtled down the cliff-face to save her. A thin line of blood veined one cheek where he'd been cut in the descent. When it healed it would look like a duelling scar, she fancied. She lifted a finger and traced it. 'I'm sorry.'

At her touch, something snapped inside him. His mouth crushed hers with a force which knocked the breath from her body, parting her unresisting lips to allow entry to his seeking tongue.

Her shirt slid up under the pressure of his hands and his fingers splayed hotly across her back. Her mind reeled and she clutched at him as warmth radiated through every part of her.

So this was how it felt to be devoured, she realised as her thoughts kaleidoscoped. Much as she tried to tell herself that she hated him, there was no denying the fascination of his arms and the power of his kiss.

She trembled with reaction as his hands found her breasts and began a mind-shattering massage which left her weak-limbed. Linking her hands behind his head, she moaned softly, her eyes fluttering closed.

As he slid his arm beneath her legs and lifted her against his chest she forced her eyes open. 'You don't... I can...'

'We'll do this my way,' he said softly, dangerously.

'When it happens'... His words returned to haunt her. It was happening now and there wasn't a thing she could do to stop it. She wasn't even sure that she wanted to try.

He carried her carefully to the sleeping-bag and set her down on it, placing a wadded sweater behind her head for a pillow. She wanted to bury her face in the soft folds but was held in thrall by his searching gaze as he looked down at her.

She made no protest when he knelt beside her, slid her jeans down over her legs and unbuttoned her shirt. Bruises were already developing where she'd slammed into the cliff-face and he explored them, frowning.

His nearness was intoxicating, the pain of the bruises nothing compared to the ache inside her as he checked her over. Without quite knowing what she was doing, she reached for him.

When his lips trailed over a bruise above her breast she gasped. Instantly his head lifted. 'Did I hurt you?'

She shook her head, her eyes misting. 'Steed.' His name came out as a tortured whisper.

His response was to take her into his mouth, his teeth teasing each nipple until she threw her head back and arched towards him. Every reason why this was wrong fled from her mind, replaced by a yearning stronger than anything in her previous experience.

He knew precisely what he was doing. Every caress, every suckling movement was a further delicious assault on her senses, until all reason fled and she clung to him, the only word left in her vocabulary his name, which she repeated over and over again.

Alarm bells rang in her head. This was madness with only one, inevitable conclusion possible. Yet the words which would make him stop stalled in her throat. Her instinctive response gave him another message entirely.

'No, please,' she finally managed to articulate, but so softly that it was a wonder he heard her.

'No, you shouldn't or no, you don't want to?' he asked in a guttural tone.

'I . . . I shouldn't.'

He trailed a line of kisses from her breasts down the length of her stomach and heard the mewing sounds of pleasure which she was powerless to withhold. 'But you want to.'

An emotional tide was racing in to engulf her. How could she deny what he could see in every quiver of nerve and muscle as he turned the full force of his powerful sexuality on her like a spotlight? Its heat threatened to consume her.

If only the spectre of Mia weren't there between them. He had no love to give, only satisfaction, and Lord knew she wanted it, however demeaning the admission might be. A part of her wanted much, much more from him but she closed her mind to this traitorous thought.

The truth hovered on her lips, a heartbeat away from expression. But he was already lifting himself away from her. 'You're forgetting another rule,' he said. 'It has to be mutual.' His fiery gaze roved over her but with clinical detachment this time.

'Never,' she vowed, bitter with the awful sense of rejection she had brought on herself and mortified to find that it hurt so much. What was happening here?

He traced a line around her jaw, trailing his fingers across her mouth in a deliberate gesture which made her gasp. 'Didn't I warn you about the futility of saying never? I could make you beg for my possession, my beautiful Linden. Would you like me to demonstrate?'

She snatched the sides of her shirt closed, her skin burning with humiliation. He knew how close she had just come to surrendering to him. Why hadn't he pressed home his advantage? 'No, I wouldn't,' she said stiffly. 'It was the nearness of the crocodile which unnerved me. It won't happen again.'

His husky laugh taunted her. 'Yes, it will. It was the nearness of a threat, I grant you, but the crocodile had nothing to do with it.'

Abruptly he turned aside. 'Stay there. I'll get something for those scratches. Where's your first-aid kit?'

'In my holdall,' she answered mechanically. Too late, she remembered what else was in the bag, but Steed was already reaching into the pocket.

The panic which shot through her mind puzzled her. Why was she afraid of Steed finding Greg's letter? Surely she should be flaunting it in front of him herself to prove his lack of power over her? Instead she felt tense and miserable, knowing Steed would think the worst. When had his opinion of her started to matter so much?

CHAPTER EIGHT

LINDEN lay frozen in place, shivering in spite of the
oven-like heat. Perhaps he would miss the crumpled
sheet of paper which lay on top of her first-aid kit.

As he lifted out the zipped case with its distinctive red cross, she held her breath, releasing it
in a ragged sigh as the note tumbled to the ground.

From where she lay, the Hamil letterhead was
plainly visible. Frowning, Steed retrieved it and
smoothed it out. 'Well, well. What have we here?'

Somehow she found the strength to gain her feet
and tried to snatch the letter but he held it away
from her. 'Why so anxious? What is it, a love letter
from Greg?'

'No, it's an apology.'

'Even more historic. Uh-uh, mustn't snatch.' His
fingers closed around her flailing wrists and he
pinned them behind her back with one hand. She
could do nothing as he scanned the few lines in
Greg's distinctive handwriting.

She felt the change come over him as he read.
His features became glacial and he made an explosive sound deep in his throat. 'Of all the cheap,
conniving women I've ever met, Linden Taylor, you
are the worst.'

His words lashed her and her eyes blurred.
'What?'

Releasing her, he stepped away then whirled on
her. 'What were you planning to do? Make love

with me then pretend I was the father of your child?'

Coldness invaded her and she felt the colour leave her face. It was an effort to summon her voice. 'I don't know what you're talking about.'

He threw the letter at her. 'Don't you? How long have you known you were carrying Greg's baby? Since the party, I imagine. Is that what you were so anxious to share with him?'

She stumbled backwards as if driven there by the force of his words. Her legs encountered a boulder and she sank on to it, horrified as she saw what conclusion he'd drawn from the letter. She pressed her hands to her face. 'I'm not pregnant by Greg or anyone else,' she forced out between her splayed fingers.

'Then why does he say it's his baby as well as yours?' His tone was unforgiving and she flinched.

Her hands slid down and she clasped them in front of her. 'He's talking about a *book* I'm trying to write. His company is interested in publishing it.' Somehow she had to make him believe her. Having him think she was capable of such deceit was painful beyond endurance.

He looked frankly sceptical. 'What kind of book, *Fun with Sex*?'

She jumped up. 'If anyone is writing the book on sex, it would be you. As it happens, mine will be about sleep therapy, to help people like your son.'

The barb went home, she saw, as his face cleared like the passing of a particularly threatening storm. He took a step towards her.

She almost wished he would stay angry with her. It was so much easier to control her rampant emotions. The memory of being in his arms was still vivid, her hastily buttoned shirt a testimony to how close he had come to possessing her entirely. A shudder shook her.

'It seems I misjudged you in this instance,' he said formally.

'It wasn't difficult, given the way the note is phrased. It was probably Greg's idea of a joke.'

Pensively, he stroked his jaw where a faint shadow darkened it. A fierce sensation like hunger gripped her and she looked away, afraid to let him see what he was doing to her.

But he knew. He came to her in swift strides, the pebbles falling away from his decisive footsteps. 'Look at me, Linden,' he commanded, his voice deeper than usual.

His fingers closed around her upper arms. She made herself look up, then wished she hadn't as she met the full brilliance of his gaze from only inches away. 'Why? So you can accuse me of more wrongdoing?' She prayed he wouldn't see through her defensiveness to the vulnerability underneath.

'It depends on how much wrong you've been doing,' he said silkily. 'Since it seems to be confession time, perhaps you should finish baring your soul to me.'

She shook her head, closing her eyes against the sensory overload she was dangerously close to feeling. 'There's nothing more to tell.'

'Isn't there?' A dangerous note had crept into his voice. 'What about the nights Greg doesn't want to see wasted?'

She'd forgotten Greg's reference to the two nights he'd spent observing the work of the sleep centre. 'We were working,' she said despairingly.

His eyes narrowed. 'Knowing Hamil, I can guess what sort of work was done.'

'Believe what you choose,' she flung at him. He would anyway. If he was angry she had a chance of resisting his powerfully male appeal. Telling him the truth was much more hazardous. 'I don't care what you think,' she finished recklessly, stunned to realise that it was no longer the whole truth.

His eyes became assessing and his palms travelled slowly up and down her arms, until tremors shook her. 'No? Then why do you tremble when I touch you?'

'Because I don't want you to touch me.' Why couldn't she make herself sound more convincing?

The stroking continued, gentle but insidious in its effect on her composure. 'Because you don't trust yourself with me?' he drawled.

It was so close to the truth that her knees buckled with shock. Only his hold on her kept her from swaying. She made a conscious effort to gather the remnants of her dignity, fighting the urge to lean into his embrace. 'How arrogant can you be, assuming that every woman you meet is just waiting to fall at your feet?'

He gave a throaty chuckle, infuriating her. 'But there are far more desirable places I'd rather have you than at my feet.'

She twisted her face to one side. 'You aren't going to *have me* anywhere.'

'Oh, no? Then it's quite safe for me to put some salve on your bruises?'

If she said no, she would be as good as admitting that she didn't trust herself with him. If she said yes, his ministrations were likely to undo all her good resolutions. 'I can do it myself, thank you,' she compromised.

Retrieving the first-aid kit, he handed her a tube of antiseptic ointment. 'Go ahead.'

Her hands shook as she applied some cream to the minor cuts she'd sustained when she'd fallen against the cliff-face. His scrutiny was unnerving. 'Do you have to stand and watch?'

'I want to be sure you do a thorough job. Even small scratches can become badly infected in the tropics and we're a long way from medical help.'

There was no denying the truth of this observation. Still, she wished he would find something better to do than stand over her as she methodically dealt with every tiny injury.

'What about the scratch on your thigh?' he asked as she was about to recap the tube.

Her face flamed. He must have seen it when he'd slid her jeans down her legs. Attending to it meant removing them again. The rock-ledge was the only place safe from crocodiles and there was nowhere else to undress in reasonable privacy.

As her head swivelled, he made a throaty noise of impatience and came to her, sweeping her into his arms to deposit her unceremoniously on to the sleeping-bag. 'I can manage,' she protested, knowing it was useless.

'Surely it's late for false modesty?' he queried, reaching for the fastening of her jeans.

It took all her self-restraint to lie passively as he removed her jeans a second time although she was quivering inwardly with a thousand emotions that she didn't dare examine too closely. It should have helped that his touch was clinical rather than romantic, but every time his fiery fingers grazed her skin her nerves jumped.

The cut was deeper than she'd realised, a sharp stone having somehow pierced the tough fabric of her jeans. She winced as he probed it to ensure that it was clean.

He heard her quick intake of breath. 'Hurting?'

She blinked away the moisture which had sprung to her eyes. 'A little. Not much.' His touch was far more devastating than the minor sting of a cut. Her pulses hammered as he massaged cream into her skin. She took refuge in humour. 'Next time you save my life, do you think you could be a little more gentle?'

He deliberately misunderstood her and she melted at the flames which leapt in the gaze he turned on her. 'So you prefer gentleness, do you? I'll bear it in mind next time.'

With that he left her to restore order to her clothing and repack the first-aid kit. There wouldn't be a next time, she vowed silently as she put the things away with savage movements. Gentle or otherwise, he wasn't coming near her again.

As it happened, there was little opportunity. The night which she'd been dreading was a literal washout when a sudden violent storm broke over their heads. They spent the night swaddled in sleeping-bags in the minimal shelter of the rock overhang while monsoon-like rains sheeted down. It was hardly an atmosphere conducive to romance. Linden refused to admit to a sense of disappointment.

Next day broke as fine and clear as if the storm had never occurred. The sky was a brilliant symphony in cerulean, the sea white-flecked and calm. Within an hour what remained of the deluge had been burned off the rocks as if it had never been.

Mudgee and his son, Mick, brought Jason back to them at lunchtime. They had passed the storm safely in a nearby cave known to Mudgee's people. They declined Steed's invitation to share a meal and melted back into the bush on silent feet.

Linden said a mental prayer of thanks for Jason, who filled the tense silence between her and Steed with chatter about his hunting trip with the aboriginals.

'Mudgee made a bait out of these straggly roots he ground up and mixed with sand. He planted it under the ledges of the rock-pools at low tide. It puts the fish to sleep so Mick and me could catch them,' he told her, his eyes shining. 'For breakfast we found wild honey and bush tomatoes. It was the coolest.' He made a face. 'I don't like eating snake, though. They toss it on to the fire till the skin's all black then pull it in half and eat it.'

She gave him a sympathetic smile. 'I wouldn't like it much either. But I'm glad you had a good time.'

His head bobbed in eager assent. 'What did you two do while I was out hunting?'

Wondering how on earth to answer him, she was relieved when Steed intervened and suggested that Jason write about his adventures for later reporting over the School of the Air. He grumbled but complied and soon had his head down over an exercise book.

Steed was brooding and solitary throughout the next leg north. Only when Linden spotted spouts of water shooting into the air every few minutes did he emerge from his shell. 'It's a whale,' he explained, manoeuvring the boat in for a closer look.

Soon she could hear the eerie whale cries and spot a calf following the vast humped shape of the mother. They travelled with the whales for some distance until the huge creatures turned seaward. By then Steed was his taciturn self again and she felt more lonely and shut out than ever.

Turning into an unnamed bay, she was surprised to see a yacht already anchored there. Three people were on shore having a barbecue. They waved when they saw *Dreamtime*.

'Do you know them?' she asked curiously.

'The yacht is the *Salamander*, owned by Janet Wong and David Eisel.'

It was indeed his old friends, she found when they took the tender in to the beach. David Eisel was a film cameraman who had crewed for Steed on some of his expeditions. He and Janet were obviously a couple, despite their differing surnames.

'You'll be interested to meet our guest,' Janet enthused, putting an arm around the second woman in the party. 'This is Kitty Barret. She's a model.'

Linden wasn't surprised. Kitty's face was a study in perfect bone-structure with skin the texture of silk. Her eye make-up should have looked out of place here, but it suited her, enhancing her enormous sea-green eyes. In deference to the burning sun she wore a wide-brimmed straw hat and a batik-printed sarong over a stunning white maillot.

'I'm an actress as well,' she explained, holding Steed's hand longer than courtesy demanded. He didn't seem to mind. 'Maybe you can use me in your next film?'

He looked interested and something died inside Linden. 'Maybe,' he agreed. 'Although there's probably a queue a mile long for your services.'

Her smile was predatory. 'I'm sure I can squeeze you in.'

Steed hadn't introduced Linden but Janet came towards her with arms outstretched. 'You must be Linden. I'm told congratulations are in order.'

David turned from rearranging meat on the barbecue. 'We heard about your engagement from the Hamils before we left Derby. Just as well I brought the champagne along.'

Linden felt her colour fade. She had managed to avoid thinking about their supposed engagement. It had only been manufactured for Greg's benefit but first Sandy, now these friends of Steed's knew about it. How much longer did he plan to keep up this absurd charade?

She looked around anxiously but Jason was climbing some rocks at the back of the beach, well out of earshot.

Janet was regarding her in concern. 'Did I say something out of turn?'

Steed moved closer, sweeping Linden into the curve of his arm. 'No, but we haven't told Jason yet and I'd rather he heard about it from us.'

'So this trip will give him a chance to get to know his future stepmother,' Janet surmised. 'What a lovely idea. Are you enjoying yourself, Linden?'

Aware that Kitty Barret was watching her keenly, she managed a tense smile. 'It's fascinating. I think I'm falling in love with the outback.'

It was true. During one restless night aboard the *Dreamtime* she had made up her mind that she wasn't going to return to Perth to live. She would have to go back to put in her resignation from the sleep clinic. What she would do afterwards she wasn't sure.

Perhaps she could get a job of some sort with the Royal Flying Doctor Service. Never had she felt so restless and unfocused, as if there was a goal she hadn't yet considered. She hoped the answer would come to her soon.

One thing was certain. She couldn't live in Derby where she might run across Steed at any time. The strain on her nerves would be excruciating. Not because he meant anything to her, she added quickly to herself. It was more a matter of self-preservation. Quite sensible really.

Somehow she joined in the gaiety of the beach barbecue, even swallowing some champagne when it was handed to her. 'To the happiness of friends,' David made the toast, careful not to spoil what he thought would be a surprise for Jason.

Steed played his part uncomfortably well. By small touches and glances he conveyed the idea that he was besotted with his bride-to-be. Knowing how patently false it was, Linden wanted to beg him to stop but was forced to endure the loving attention.

'How did you two meet?' Janet asked as they sprawled on the sand after lunch.

'At Greg Hamil's engagement party,' Steed told the literal truth. 'I'd seen her from afar in Perth and couldn't believe it when Lin arrived in Derby in need of an escort.'

Kitty gave her a searching look. 'Some people have all the luck.'

He favoured Linden with a warm smile which made her want to lash out at him. 'You don't need luck when you have other gifts, as Linden has.'

As no doubt he planned, this engendered a round of slightly ribald teasing, carefully veiled out of consideration for Jason's tender years. Linden was furious at the way Steed managed to convince his friends that theirs was a passionate affair.

'How could you?' she snapped in an undertone as they started back towards the tender.

'Careful, you'll blow your image,' he murmured, his arm curving around her shoulder.

At his touch she tensed, but dared not shrug him off in case they were being watched. 'I don't care for an image as your... your *sexual plaything*.'

'It's hardly play,' he reproved, directing his words into her ear so that it looked as if he was whispering endearments. 'I was simply demonstrating the degree of intimacy expected of an engaged couple.'

'An intimacy which is completely false,' she snapped back, finding the very thought a threat to her peace of mind. Surely she didn't want it to be any other way?

Before they reached the tender, Janet caught up with them. 'Kitty needs to get back to Derby to go to a modelling job and we still have a way to go. Do you think she could hitch a ride with you?'

Linden's heart sank. She should be delighted to have the other woman aboard to deflect Steed's attention from herself, but for some unfathomable reason the idea made her acutely miserable.

Kitty was hovering behind Janet, confidently awaiting his enthusiastic response. 'It would be a tight squeeze,' he said after a moment's thought. 'Linden and Jason have the spare cabins.'

Janet smiled. 'I seem to recall that the master cabin aboard *Dreamtime* is a double. Couldn't Linden bunk in with you, leaving a single cabin for Kitty?'

'It's a thought.'

Linden's stomach lurched. He couldn't possibly mean her to share his cabin with him? Damn Steed for giving his friends the impression that such an arrangement was acceptable to her.

'I'm afraid I'm a restless sleeper,' she protested to Janet.

Kitty's feline gaze lightened and she rested an elegant hand on Steed's arm. 'I could always share your double cabin,' she volunteered.

He gave her a smile which managed to convey regret that he had to refuse. 'It's a delightful idea but not really practical in the circumstances. Linden will gladly change cabins, won't you, darling?'

There was nothing Linden could do but smile through clenched teeth and nod in agreement. Her mind was already racing over the alternatives. Wherever she slept on the way back to Derby, it was not going to be in his bed.

But it seemed she was worrying needlessly. While David took Kitty back to the *Salamander* to fetch her things, Steed assured Linden that the situation was under control.

'You may think so, but I don't call being forced to share your cabin a satisfactory solution,' she stated.

'A pity. It would have been interesting.'

Would have been? 'Then you don't——'

'I'll sleep on the floor of Jason's cabin,' he cut in. 'You can have the master suite to yourself.'

As a solution it should have satisfied her but she was left with a leaden feeling of disappointment. It made no sense at all but it plagued her for the rest of the day.

Kitty wasted no time in making herself at home aboard *Dreamtime*. She seemed to have an enormous amount of luggage which filled the cabin she took over from Linden and spilled into Steed's cabin as well.

She soon made it clear that she didn't wash dishes—'I have to take care of my hands, you know'—and she didn't cook. This left Linden with most of the chores. Evidently the state of her hands was less critical.

Kitty's hands were quite safe when it came to helping Steed with any of his tasks. The actress-model was knowledgeable about film-making and they spent long sessions discussing technical matters which left Linden silent and brooding.

Whenever he needed a model to give a potential scene perspective and scale she posed happily for his still camera. 'It looks as if I'll have to put Kitty on the payroll,' he announced after one such session.

'I thought that was her intention,' Linden said sourly.

His eyebrows lifted. 'Jealous, Linden?'

She gave the sandwiches she was making much closer attention than they deserved. 'You're implying that I care what you do or with whom.'

She was achingly aware that he had moved closer behind her. His breath lifted the fine hairs on the back of her neck. 'We are engaged,' he reminded her gruffly.

Her knife savaged a tomato, the seeds spilling on to her hands. 'Only in public, as I'm sure Miss Australia has worked out.'

His angry response quivered between them. 'You saw fit to tell her?'

She turned wounded eyes to him. 'No, I... You haven't been very attentive to me, that's all. It wouldn't be hard for her to work out the truth.'

As she met his eyes and saw the purposeful gleam in them, panic struck her. Why on earth had she made such a provocative statement?

He took the knife from her trembling fingers and set it down on the chopping board. Lifting her hand, he began to lick the tomato residue from her fingers. 'Steed,' she whispered. 'Please...'

'I'm following your suggestion—paying you more attention,' he murmured, his lips moving against her fingertips. As he sucked gently on her index finger, her stomach muscles spasmed and she drew in her breath.

'I didn't mean——'

He silenced her by brushing his lips across hers. She tasted tomato mixed with the salty male taste of his mouth. Her back was to the galley and he took up most of the narrow walkway so she was pressed against him. He felt hot and incredibly masculine.

Her breasts were crushed against his hair-strewn chest where his shirt hung open. Her nipples went on instant alert and her breathing quickened.

'What if Jason sees us?' she managed, over-whelmed by the assault on her senses which showed no signs of abating.

'It will be good for his education. Save me going over all that birds and bees stuff.'

It was an education for her too, but not one she welcomed. His kiss was a lesson in submission and mastery as he commanded her lips to open to him. Then he proceeded to teach her about the erogenous zones of the soft palate, although the lesson was lost in a mist of bewildering sensations which left her reeling.

Her blood roared in her ears and she wondered if she was about to faint for the first time in her life. Clinging to him, she felt the powerful rise and fall of his chest as his breathing deepened. The lesson wasn't entirely one-sided, she realised dazedly.

'Steed, where did you put those green filters? Oops!' Kitty blundered into the cabin. Anyone else would have made a graceful retreat but she perched on the wooden steps leading from the deck, her arms folded. She looked amused. 'I didn't know you did CPR, Steed. I'll keep it in mind in case I need mouth-to-mouth resuscitation myself.'

Without releasing Linden, he said over his shoulder, 'This is a private lesson, Kitty. I'll see you up on deck in a few minutes.'

A sensation of triumph stole over Linden, although she wondered at its source. Kitty's arms dropped to her sides and she smiled without warmth. 'Whatever you say, Skipper. I gather lunch will be a while.' She turned to go back on deck but not before she shot Linden a look of such malevolence that she was shaken.

Instead of convincing Kitty that he and Linden were indeed engaged, Steed's demonstration had created a new difficulty. It was obvious now that Kitty hated her and she had the uncomfortable feeling that the model would make a formidable enemy.

She writhed in Steed's arms, wishing he hadn't chosen this moment to claim his rights as her so-called fiancé. Apart from playing havoc with Linden's peace of mind, his attention meant that she now had Kitty's opposition to contend with. She wasn't sure which complication disturbed her the most.

CHAPTER NINE

LINDEN needn't have worried. After Steed's lesson in the confines of the galley, he saw no further need to demonstrate that he and Linden were lovebirds. Or so she concluded when he paid her no further amorous attention as they retraced their route south along the Kimberley coast.

Her feelings were in serious conflict. She hadn't enjoyed his attention, she assured herself fiercely, yet perversely she missed it when he left her alone. The heat must be affecting her reasoning, she concluded.

Kitty had no such difficulty. She seemed to regard Steed as a greater challenge than ever. Whenever Linden looked around there was Kitty, draped elegantly over the boat, quizzing Steed about his work with breathless interest. Linden she treated as little more than a galley slave. She wasn't averse to issuing orders when it suited her. But a request for Linden to do some laundry for her was too much. 'The last time I did any laundry at the water's edge, Steed had to save me from a crocodile,' she said in an imitation of Kitty's breathless tones. 'He was extremely forceful about forbidding me to do it again.'

'Hmm.' Kitty stalked off, clutching the offending garments.

Linden wondered about her own motives. She should have refused the task with quiet dignity.

What had possessed her to bring Steed into it? She knew it was a sure way to provoke the other woman. What was going on here? It wasn't as if she wanted to stake a claim to him, was it?

As penance she tried to be nicer to Kitty although it took every ounce of grit and determination. The model was a graduate of the 'give her an inch and she'll take a mile' school. By the time Linden retired to her cabin that night she was exhausted.

Steed's cabin was comfortable, with a full-sized double bed, but tonight it seemed lonely rather than spacious. Her head turned towards the other half of the bed, almost as if she was wishing... No. She sat up with a jolt. This pretend engagement was preying on her mind. Why else would she be thinking such betraying thoughts?

Too restless to sleep although she was tired, she slipped on a robe and brushed her hair back. Leaving her feet bare for coolness, she opened the door leading to the deck and stepped out into the balmy night air.

Gossamer clouds scudded past overhead, crisscrossed by the serrated outline of fruit bats which colonised the trees all along the coast. Their high-pitched squeals reached her ears from the shoreline along with the occasional barking cough of a crocodile calling to its fellows.

The night sky made her catch her breath in wonder. The stars were much brighter than down south, their brilliance punctuated by satellites and shooting stars streaking past. In the shadow of the bridge she leaned against the bulkhead and allowed the vista to calm her.

Feeling better, she decided to have a cool drink before trying to sleep. About to descend the wooden steps leading to the saloon, she froze. In the walkway beyond the galley, someone was moving about.

She stood rooted to the spot as Steed's broad-shouldered figure emerged from Jason's cabin. He closed the door softly and went to the cabin which had belonged to Linden and was now Kitty's, where he tapped on the door.

Linden held her breath as the door opened to reveal Kitty clad in a diaphanous black négligé through which her shapely model's figure was clearly outlined against the light. There was an exchange which Linden failed to catch then he slipped into Kitty's cabin.

Linden's knuckles whitened as she gripped the door-frame. Steed visiting Kitty's cabin late at night? The discovery shouldn't surprise her since the model had practically thrown herself at him since she'd come aboard. But it did. A shaft of pain stabbed her. Kitty's clothes were hardly designed for discussing business.

Reeling back on to the deck, Linden gulped great lungfuls of air, trying to still the frantic pounding of her heart. She felt as if an attack was imminent but knew the cause wasn't so easily defined. Her heart was certainly in danger but not for any medical reason. Her suffering was due to a cause which had been obvious for days, needing only the courage to be faced. She was in love with Steed.

Facing it didn't make the discovery any less disastrous. It only explained why she reacted so strongly every time he came near her, and why seeing him go to Kitty made Linden's fingernails itch for some target practice.

How could she have been so blind? Or so stupid as to let it happen? she asked herself, sinking on to a deck chair and staring at the shadowy outline of the shore.

But had she let herself fall in love? What could she have done to prevent it, even knowing that Steed didn't return her love? A casual fling with Kitty to satisfy his male urges was probably justifiable, but anything deeper was a betrayal of his love for Mia. Linden had never felt more bereft.

How long she sat there she had no idea but finally exhaustion overcame her and she returned to her cabin. She had no memory of a sad dream but her pillow was damp when she awakened.

It was late by the time she arose. She would have given a lot to be able to remain in her cabin. The thought of facing Steed was almost more than she could bear. But Jason was eager to have her join the others aboard the tender for the trip to shore. There was no way to avoid it without arousing comment.

When she saw the landing site she wished she had made some excuse to remain on board. 'Why have we come back here?' she asked tensely, surveying the rock-ledge where Steed had so nearly made love to her after her brush with the crocodile.

His eyes glowed, daring her to remember. 'I hadn't finished surveying the top of the waterfall when you had need of my attention.'

As late as yesterday, recalling how he had attended her would have brought a flush of pleasure to her cheeks. Now, knowing how he had passed the night and with whom, Linden wished she could erase the memory of his kisses and the feel of his hands on her exposed flesh. But the memories refused to retreat, instead threatening to swamp her with their bittersweetness.

Jason elected to climb the waterfall with his father. 'I'll rest on the rocks in the shade,' she volunteered.

'As long as you stay away from the water's edge.'

'Don't worry, I will.' There was no way she wanted a repeat of the earlier scene.

Kitty stretched indolently. 'I think I'll stay too. It's too hot for physical exertion—at least of the aerobic variety.' Her smile favoured Steed, hinting at the kind of exercise she would prefer to indulge in with him.

He smiled back, unperturbed. 'To each her own, Kitty. Try to behave yourself while I'm gone.'

Kitty's feline look made Linden feel ill. 'It's easy to behave myself when you're *gone*. It's when you're not that I have a problem.'

'Force yourself,' he said shortly, and led Jason towards the cliff-face.

'Sooner them than me.' Kitty stretched her long legs out in front of her and began to apply sunscreen lotion with great concentration.

A vivid image of Steed applying the cream for her made Linden choke back a sob. The small sound made Kitty look up. 'Is something the matter?'

'I didn't get much sleep last night. I feel terrible this morning.'

Without lifting her head, Kitty said, 'It must be the strain of keeping up your act.'

'My what?'

'Pretending to be the love of Steed's life. Last night he told me...' She covered her mouth in mock-distress. 'But I mustn't speak out of turn.'

The bottom dropped out of Linden's world. How could he make her the subject of pillow-talk between him and Kitty? 'He told you?'

'Not in so many words, but anyone can see you two aren't the ideal engaged couple. How did you get him to propose—pretend to be pregnant?'

'It's hardly your affair, is it?' she said with icy dignity although she was falling apart inside.

Kitty looked thoughtful. 'Funny you should use the word "affair". It rather fits, doesn't it?'

How many more nights had Steed spent in Kitty's cabin? Linden's anguish was mirrored on her face and Kitty patted her hand. 'Don't look so mortified. Men like Steed are highly sexed. They need more than kisses and cuddles to satisfy them.'

Was that the problem? If she had given herself to him, would things be different? He had rejected her, she recalled unhappily. She had blamed it on his loyalty to Mia but perhaps the lack was in herself.

'I see you're giving it some thought. Wise move. I'd hate you to be here when I come back to Derby after my modelling assignment.'

At the model's blithe assumption that she could usurp Linden's place without opposition, steel stiffened her spine. Her love might not be returned but she was not going to be ordered out of Steed's life by Kitty. 'It's hardly your decision, is it?' she returned smoothly.

Surprise glittered in Kitty's green eyes. 'Where's your pride? Surely you aren't waiting until *Steed* asks you to go?'

'Since he hasn't yet, the question is academic.'

Kitty ran a hand down her silken leg, emphasising the shapely length of it. 'There are other issues to consider. Jason doesn't know about your so-called engagement, does he? I gather he was attached to his mother.'

An icy feeling invaded Linden. 'What are you saying?'

'Just that it's probably time he was told.'

To Linden's horror, Jason chose that moment to rejoin them, ferreting in the Esky for a cool drink. 'Dad's on his way down,' he informed them, drinking thirstily.

Linden saw Kitty's smile and everything in her shrieked a protest at what she knew the model planned to do. 'No, please,' she begged.

Kitty's smile was unconvincing. 'Isn't it great to have a new mother, Jason?'

He looked confused. 'Linden isn't my mother. She's my friend.'

'Kitty, please.'

There was no stopping her. 'But she's going to be your mother as soon as she marries your father. Won't it be cosy?'

As his face contorted in protest, Linden reached for him but he shrugged her hand away. 'Why didn't you tell me? You don't care what I think, do you?'

Before she could gather her wits, he dropped the drink and ran off towards the creek mouth, plunging headlong into the undergrowth as if pursued by demons.

'Dear me, he doesn't seem to like the idea,' Kitty observed, sounding shaken at the effect she'd provoked.

Linden pushed her aside to scramble after Jason. 'Tell Steed which way he went. I've got to go after him; there could be crocodiles in there.'

There was no sign of Jason in the clearing beyond the creek entrance and she looked around frantically. Which way had he gone?

Steed caught up with her as she ventured along a sandbank. 'What the blazes do you think you're doing?'

'Jason ran in here. I had to come after him. It's my fault that he ran away.'

He looked frighteningly angry. 'It's debatable but our first priority is to find him.' Dropping to his haunches, he scanned the length of the sandbank while she quivered with impatience.

'Shouldn't we get going? He'll be miles away.'

He pointed towards a wide ditch cutting through the sand-flats. 'His tracks go along there.'

The sand was criss-crossed with crab tracks and debris. She could see no trace of human footprints. 'How can you be sure?'

'I learned a thing or two from my aboriginal friends,' he explained as he set off.

Keeping up with him demanded all her attention. Like a raging bull he charged through stands of spiky pandanus palms and across dried-up gullies where paperbark trees leaned precariously towards the north and lilies clustered in the shallows.

At one point their progress was halted as a green tree snake slithered along a branch. Supported by a powerful tail, it moved from branch to branch, weaving its way higher into the leaves. Linden looked nervously upwards as they passed beneath it.

Steed's arm came around her. 'Relax. They're completely harmless.'

Some of his strength flowed into her. 'How much further can Jason have gone?'

'Not much. His tracks say he's tiring. We'll catch up with him in a few minutes.'

What could she say to him when they did? She could hardly believe Kitty's heartlessness, using a small boy as a pawn in her game. She hoped Steed didn't think Linden herself capable of such a terrible thing. Her heart ached for Jason and for the agony Steed must be enduring as they searched for his son. He gave no sign of what he must be feeling but his jaw was set as he helped her over slippery rocks and deep patches of boggy sand. The heat was becoming unbearable but she was determined to press on until they found Jason.

Suddenly a clearing appeared, surrounded by a wall of sandstone. A natural hollow was visible a couple of metres from the ground. Broken pieces of rock led like steps up to the cave entrance.

'Do you think he's inside?' she asked fearfully.

'His tracks end at the rocks. This must be the cave where Mudgee took them to shelter from the storm. It's used for initiation rites.'

She started for the rock steps but Steed restrained her. 'You can't go in. It's forbidden to women.'

'But Jason may be hurt. This is no time for stupid superstition.'

'You don't have to like it; just wait here while I go in and fetch him.'

Frustration gnawed at her but she dared not risk his wrath any further by venturing inside the cave. She would never forgive herself if Jason had been hurt because of her.

She almost cried with relief when Steed appeared at the cave mouth. His arm was across Jason's shoulder and the boy was all right.

He climbed down to her shamefaced. 'Dad says I have to apologise to you for running off.'

Yearning to envelop him in a bone-rattling hug, she pressed her arms to her sides. He had already shown that he didn't welcome motherly affection from her. 'It's all right, Jason. I know you were upset.' Her gaze swung to Steed in mute appeal. 'I didn't tell him, I swear.'

'I'd already guessed it was Kitty. I've made Jason understand that nobody's betraying the memory of his mother. She'll always have a special place in his heart.'

And in Steed's she assumed, feeling her own heart shatter into tiny little pieces. Her legs gave way and she collapsed on to a sandstone boulder.

Steed handed her a flask from a pouch at his waist. 'Drink this. You'll feel better.'

She regarded it dubiously. 'What is it?'

'Water. The elixir of life in the tropics.'

She drank thirstily, feeling the drops slide down her throat like the sweetest honey. She'd hardly noticed how much she'd been perspiring as they'd forced their way through the undergrowth. Reaching Jason before any harm befell him had kept her going.

A stinging sensation near her ankle drew her attention and she recoiled as she encountered a black slug-like creature adhering to her calf. Recoiling, she let out a scream.

Jason laughed. 'It's only a leech. Dad will get it off you. They don't hurt...much.'

His ghoulish schoolboy humour was no help. She was trembling as Steed rolled back the cuff of her jeans and slid her sock down to expose her ankle.

She shuddered as he grasped the creature between thumb and forefinger and carefully removed it. 'It may bleed for a while but they do no harm. Modern doctors are rediscovering the value of leeches in everyday medical practice.'

'I think I'll pass,' she said shakily. She was becoming disturbingly aware of Steed on his knees before her, his bent head so close that she yearned to thread her fingers through his hair and pull his sculpted head up to hers. His hands on her ankle were gentle as he replaced her sock and rolled her jeans down.

His head lifted and his eyes met hers so that she was forced to veil the pain which filled them. 'You'll be fine now.'

It would be a long time before she was fine again but she kept the thought to herself. She was well aware that Steed's allegiance belonged elsewhere. And Jason had made his feelings about her as a prospective stepmother abundantly clear.

She blinked hard and stood up. 'Thanks.'

'I'll check your ankles again before we go back aboard. I should have warned you about leeches.'

He should have warned her about a lot of things, like the dangers of falling in love with him, she told herself as they set off towards the shore.

Now the danger to Jason was over her heightened senses made her acutely aware of her environment. She noticed a flock of black cockatoos squabbling and screeching in the trees, oblivious of their presence. As they reached the sand-flats, curlews and other marsh birds waded ahead of them and ibises called out as they flocked from the mangroves.

If not for the ache in her heart, she would have revelled in being this close to nature. Not even the possibility of crocodiles, for which Steed was ever vigilant, could diminish the magic of the raw beauty surrounding her.

Kitty rushed up to them as they emerged on to the rock-ledge. 'Jason, you poor child. When I saw you run off like that, I could have killed myself for opening my stupid mouth.'

She turned tear-filled eyes to Steed. 'Can you forgive me for being so insensitive?'

He brushed aside her apologies. 'Jason is fine so there's no harm done.'

'But when I think what could have happened . . .' She closed her eyes and leaned back against the rock-face.

Linden saw his eyes tighten. 'Fortunately it didn't. But I suggest you monitor your words more carefully in the future.'

Opening her eyes, Kitty nodded contritely. 'Of course, Steed. You know I'll do everything in my power to make it up to you.'

Fairly sure of what the offer might include, Linden turned away to conceal the pain which radiated through her. Would he have been so understanding if Linden had been the one at fault? Somehow she doubted it. She was only too well aware of the limits of his tolerance where she was concerned.

For the remainder of the journey she kept to herself as much as possible. Several times she surprised Jason regarding her with ill-concealed curiosity and she longed to tell him that he had no cause for concern. There was no chance of her taking his mother's place in any capacity, because she wasn't really engaged to his father.

It was odd that Steed hadn't made the point himself now that there was little opportunity for her to come between Greg and Sandra. He must have his own reasons for keeping up the charade, she surmised. Was he still sleeping with Kitty? Being engaged would allow him to dictate the terms of their relationship.

'Penny for them,' he observed, startling her by coming up behind her on the afterdeck.

Her eyes stung with tears but she blinked them away. She didn't want him to see how his presence shattered her peace of mind. Letting him think she was still heart-whole was her last defence.

'My thoughts aren't worth that much,' she denied, irritated with herself for sounding so husky.

He rested lean forearms on the guardrail and stared out to sea. 'Still holding it against me for making you come along on this trip?'

What was she supposed to say—that she was glad he had made her fall in love with a man who had no interest in loving her? That she masochistically enjoyed imagining him spending every night in Kitty's cabin?

This was the first time he'd caught her alone since Jason had run away, and her body felt super-charged with the sense of his nearness. Working on board, he wore only a loose cotton shirt left open for coolness, over cut-off jeans which frayed tantalisingly across his broad thighs. She held herself rigid against the pain of wanting to touch him and knowing she had no right.

'What do you think?' she asked, her voice as taut as a violin string.

'I think you've enjoyed yourself more than you want to admit,' he observed.

His perceptiveness made her stifle a gasp. 'You flatter yourself. I'm merely making the best of a difficult situation.'

'You still think of being engaged to me as a difficult situation?'

Controlling her breathing had never been more of a challenge. 'But I'm not engaged to you, am I?'

He gave a sardonic chuckle. 'A great many people think of you as my fiancée.'

Her eyes flashed fire. 'Their numbers don't include Kitty Barret, surely?'

'Because she knows I don't share your cabin at night?'

Yes, because you share hers, her anguished heart answered. Aloud she said, 'She's well aware that we aren't the usual starry-eyed engaged couple.'

'She also thinks I share Jason's cabin because of his night terrors,' he said in a clipped voice.

'Although fortunately there have been no recurrences since we left Winjana.'

So he hadn't spent every night with Kitty, she thought, and hastily checked the warmth which surged through her. It didn't matter. She didn't matter—to him. 'I'm glad your strategy worked—with Jason,' she added before he could misconstrue her comment. 'I'd hate to think I was sacrificed for no good purpose.'

'Poor Linden,' he murmured, with a hint of steel in the soft words. 'A sacrificial lamb for everybody. Surely it hasn't all been pure torture?'

Thinking of the moments when he'd held her and kissed her, when he'd massaged healing cream into her limbs, she was forced to shake her head. 'I've enjoyed seeing the outback,' she admitted, keeping the rest to herself.

'But you're still pining for Hamil, is that it?' His harsh interpretation of her reticence came as a stinging shock.

'Of course not.' In truth, she'd hardly thought of Greg for days. It was Steed himself who dominated her thoughts now.

His grip tightened on the guardrail. 'We'll soon see, won't we? We're to have dinner with Greg and Sandra the night we get back, after we transfer Kitty to the supply boat so Ernest can take her back to the mainland.'

How could she survive another evening of pretending to be his fiancée under the knowing eye of his cousin? 'Can't you go to dinner with them alone?'

'No,' he denied. 'I'm not leaving you alone in the house while Greg's on the island.'

So he was still taking no chances with his cousin's happiness. He was determined to keep up appearances, no matter what the cost to her peace of mind. But how could she sustain her role without betraying her true feelings, even for one more night?

CHAPTER TEN

BY THE time they were due to dine with Greg and Sandra, Linden's nerves were in shreds. She had survived the return trip to Winjana by will-power alone, keeping a tight rein on her feelings every step of the way.

She almost came undone when it was time to see Kitty aboard the supply boat. 'I'll be back as soon as I finish my assignment,' the model assured Steed. Draping herself around him, she pressed her lips to his in much more than a farewell salute, which made Linden want to scream.

Steed hadn't minded, she noticed bitterly. He was positively cheerful as he helped the woman aboard Ernest's boat and settled her amid her mountain of luggage. No doubt he was anticipating her return with equal enthusiasm. By then Linden would be safely back in Perth and there would be no further impediments to their passion.

She tried to tell herself they were well-matched but her own desires gave the lie to it. She wanted him too much herself to be charitable about him and Kitty.

'Will Jason be coming with us to the Hamilses?' she asked, keeping her tone carefully level as they returned to his house.

'He's spending the night at Chloe's. By the time he finishes telling Terry about his adventures, I doubt if he'll get much sleep at all.'

He wasn't the only one. She hadn't counted on spending the night alone with Steed but his refusal to let her leave on the supply boat made it inevitable.

'What should I wear to dinner tonight?' she asked, to defuse her growing tension. Having spent the last few days in jeans and shirts, she found it an effort to think in terms of more civilised clothing.

'I'm sure Sandra has something suitable in her wardrobe,' he supplied.

'Such as sackcloth and ashes?'

She regretted the taunt when she saw his face darken. 'Don't even think of causing a scene. Remember I'll be at your side the whole evening and you'll be leaving with me when it's over. Once we're alone you'll be accountable to me for your behaviour.'

'I'm not Jason. You can't turn me over your knee,' she threw at him, her tone mutinous.

His answering glare swept over her. 'Care to test our theory?'

The steel in his tone should have warned her to tread warily but she was too emotionally over-wrought to heed it. 'Go ahead, bully me into sub-mission. You've done nothing else since the moment we met.'

Panic flared through her as he advanced on her, his expression grimly purposeful. Dear Lord, what had she invited with her rash taunt? Her faltering backward steps brought her up against a tree with nowhere left to run. He continued his relentless advance until she was angled against the rough bark, held fast by his hands on either side of her head, his weight pinning her in place.

'I've never had to bully you into submission,' he said, his eyes flashing dangerously. 'All I've had to do is this.' He kissed her hard, his mouth sealing to hers with pitiless precision.

Her control began to slip away. Why had she provoked him into a fight that she knew she couldn't possibly win? All he had to do was kiss her and he might as well brand her for life. Humiliation welled through her. He was right. No bullying was needed when the touch of his lips could bend her effortlessly to his will.

When he lifted his head, her eyes were bright. 'Why didn't you let me leave with Kitty?'

'Because I'm not ready,' he bit out. 'We have some unfinished business.'

Oh, yes, she was still to be paraded in front of Greg and Sandra, being shown off as a prized possession which need trouble his cousin no longer. He released her and she slammed into her room, collapsing on to the bed. She refused to cry for him yet her eyes ached with tears. How much more of this could she endure?

Emotionally exhausted, she must have fallen asleep because it was twilight when she stirred. Contrarily, she ignored Sandra's clothes in favour of her own. She had brought only one dressy outfit and defiance made her drag it out. It was a two-piece outfit of satin halter which buttoned to one side, leaving her back and shoulders bare, over a slim-fitting black miniskirt. The periwinkle satin flattered her blonde-auburn hair and the skirt made her legs look long and slender. It was probably better suited to a disco in Perth than dinner on an island but she needed the confidence-booster of looking as good as she possibly could.

Her make-up carefully applied, she dressed and slid her feet into low-heeled black sandals. A touch of Arpège perfume completed her preparations. She inspected herself critically in the mirror. From her outward appearance Steed would never guess that she was falling apart inside.

When she emerged he was waiting with a cool drink for her. 'You look lovely,' he commented, his eyes lingering on the revealing halter which made it quite plain that she wore no bra underneath. 'But it won't work.'

The drink almost slipped from her fingers. 'What won't work?'

'Your rather blatant attempt to show Greg what he's missing.'

Seething inwardly, she drank the aperitif quickly. 'Have you considered it may not be Greg I want to show?'

'Thank your stars we have to leave now or I might make you pay for that remark.'

'Violence, Steed? I thought you were too big a man to use brute strength on a woman.'

'Will it take another lesson to prove I don't need to use brute strength on you? My methods are much subtler.'

She swallowed hard, her imagination moving into overdrive. Dressed in a cream pilot's shirt and tan linen trousers, he looked every inch the man she'd fallen in love with, but she didn't want him to take her to prove a point. She retreated as gracefully as she could. 'Isn't it time for us to go?'

'I'm sure Sandra and Greg won't mind if we're a little late and a touch dishevelled,' he said with mocking emphasis.

His laughter followed her as she scooted out of the door and down the path towards the Hamil compound. Only one of the houses was lighted and Sandra came out on to the elevated deck to greet them. 'Come on up. I thought you'd never get here.'

How young and carefree she sounded, Linden thought with a touch of envy. She pasted a smile on her lips and tried not to tense too much when Steed tucked her hand into the crook of his arm to ascend the staircase to the deck.

The Hamil house was simply designed but elegant. The deck opened off an open-plan living area, accessible by a wall of sliding glass which offered a breathtaking view all the way to the distant islands of the archipelago. By night the outlook was of velvet darkness lit by the phosphorescence capping the waves and the lights of distant vessels at sea. Overhead the stars twinkled, seemingly close enough to touch.

It was a setting for love and romance, Linden thought bleakly. Sandra had made the most of it by setting a table close to the wall of glass. The table, topped with a single slab of marble, was set with casual napery and silverware. Champagne glistened in a silver ice bucket, awaiting their arrival.

'What's the occasion?' she asked, noting the costly French label on the champagne.

Sandra exchanged glances with Steed. 'You haven't told her our secret?'

'I thought you'd prefer to make the announcement yourselves.'

Linden's puzzled look went from Sandra to Greg then settled on Steed. 'What's this all about?'

Greg finished pouring the amber liquid and passed a glass to each of them. 'I told Steed by Rad-phone, but no one else knows. Sandra and I were married yesterday. We're officially on our honeymoon.'

The reason for Sandra's glowing expression became clear. Also obvious was Steed's motive in forcing her to attend this dinner. He wanted to make it clear that Sandra's claim on Greg was absolute.

She submitted to Sandra's embrace feeling uncomfortable, but the other woman was too euphoric to notice. 'I know this is a surprise, but there was no one else we wanted to share the celebration with,' she explained, including Linden in the smile she shone on Steed.

Steed sipped the champagne. 'I take it the family still doesn't know?'

Sandra moved into the circle of Greg's arms. 'Not a word. I'm not looking forward to the music we'll have to face but it was our choice.'

'Sandra wanted to marry me, not the scion of Hamil Incorporated,' Greg explained.

Linden could almost hear Steed's thoughts: unlike certain gold-diggers he could name. A shiver shook her. No doubt he thought her pallor was due to Greg's announcement, when the strain of pretending to be Steed's fiancé was much greater.

They sat down to a meal of chilled mango soup followed by fillets of barramundi in mushroom sauce, and a tangy strawberry sorbet. Sandra had prepared most of the food ahead of time so that she could join in the conversation.

Luckily Steed did most of the talking for them both, while Linden played with her food, her appetite gone. Now that Greg and Sandra were safely married, he had no reason to keep her on the island. This must be the point he had brought her here to make, before putting her on the first flight back to Perth tomorrow. She should be relieved at the prospect of returning to her old life, but all she could think of was the agony of parting from Steed, probably forever.

She declined Sandra's offer of more dessert. 'No, thank you, I couldn't.'

Sandra looked concerned. 'You've hardly eaten a thing. Are you sure you feel all right?'

Linden was aware of Steed's cool appraisal. She could almost feel the aura of annoyance he was projecting towards her. He thought she was unhappy over Greg's marriage. She made an effort to participate more fully in the discussion over coffee.

'Much better,' he murmured to her as he passed her a fresh cup of the aromatic New Guinea blend.

The cup rattled in its saucer as she accepted it. 'What do you mean?'

'At least you're trying to look as if this marriage is good news.'

'I am happy about it,' she insisted, knowing he was unlikely to believe her. 'Greg and Sandra seem very well-suited.'

His fingers closed around her wrist in an apparently playful gesture. Only she felt the steel in his grasp. 'They *are* well-suited so you can forget any schemes you might be hatching to spoil things.'

'I have no such plans so your warning is totally unnecessary,' she said in an undertone.

His fingers grazed the pulse-point at her wrist and his eyes gleamed as he registered the extent of her inner turmoil. 'I think it's very necessary. You're wound as tightly as a coiled spring.'

But not for the reason he thought. She shook off his hand and stood up. 'Excuse me. I need to get some fresh air. I have a slight headache.'

Sandra looked anxious. 'Can I get you something for it?'

'No, I'll be fine. Please finish your coffee. I'm sure some fresh air is all I need.' She was aware of Steed's assessing look as she escaped on to the deck.

She had no idea how long she'd been outside when there was a movement behind her. She tensed, steeling herself for further reproach from Steed. But it was Greg who joined her.

'Feeling better?'

'A little. It's a beautiful night.'

He rested his forearms on the timber balustrade and stared out to sea. 'I meant what I said in my letter about owing you an apology.'

'I got it, but there's no need.'

'Yes, there is. In many ways you helped Sandy and me decide to jump into marriage.'

Her eyes widened. 'She knows about me?'

In the shadowy light spilling from the room she saw him nod. 'She's an amazing woman, probably better than I deserve. She knows I've always had the family to fall back on for everything. I've never needed to take responsibility for anything. The thought of taking on a commitment like marriage scared me senseless.'

'So you started seeing me in the hope that Sandra would break it off,' she guessed.

'I was using you. I'm sorry about that too.'

'I'm not thrilled about it but I think I understand. I'm glad it worked out for the best.' She meant it. Despite what Steed thought, she wished the couple well.

He offered her his hand. 'Friends?'

She took it. 'Of course.'

A rustling sound underneath the deck made her start. Greg felt her tremor. 'It's only fruit bats.' He covered her hand with his free one. 'I also meant what I wrote about our other project, if you're still interested.'

A clean break still seemed wiser. 'No, Greg. If the book is ever published, it won't be by you. Sandra's patience isn't infinite. You'll need to earn her trust.'

He released her long enough to reach into his wallet and extract a business card. 'Here's my private number at the office in case you change your mind.' He gave a self-deprecating laugh. 'You're right about Sandra's patience. She's threatened to cut me into little pieces if I put one foot off the straight and narrow, but she wouldn't mind a business arrangement.'

Linden managed to smile. 'I think not, Greg.'

With a rueful grin, he went back inside.

Footsteps broke the stillness close beside her and she started, the card fluttering to the deck. 'Who's there? Is it you, Greg?' she demanded.

Steed loomed out of the darkness. 'Sorry to disappoint you.' He retrieved the fallen card. 'I think you dropped this.'

She extended her hand for it. 'I did, thank you.'

He pocketed it instead. 'You won't be needing it.'

He was insufferable. 'How do you know?'

'Because he's a married man. Or didn't it occur to you when he invited you to meet him?'

'It couldn't possibly be about business, I suppose?'

'Ah, yes, the book. Clever of him to use it as bait.'

'He isn't using it as anything of the sort,' she said, hoping it was true. She had no intention of calling Greg anyway but she was damned if she'd tell Steed and let him think he'd browbeaten her into agreeing.

'Then you're going to him in spite of everything?'

'I'll let you know when I make up my mind.'

With measured steps he advanced on her. 'Perhaps I should help you to decide.'

Behind her was a second set of steps leading to the ground. She fled down them but he was quicker, vaulting over the railing to land lightly on the path in front of her. 'In a hurry to get to your lesson?' he drawled.

Adrenalin coursed through her. 'I'm in a hurry to get to bed,' she snapped.

It was the wrong thing to say, she knew as soon as she saw the answering glint in his eyes. 'My sentiments exactly.' Before she could protest he slid a hand under her knees and lifted her against his chest.

They were halfway back to his house before she found the breath to protest. 'Put me down. What will Greg and Sandra think if we just disappear?'

'I've told them I'm taking you home to bed—and I am.'

It was where she wanted to be more than anything in the world, but not like this. His long-legged stride brought them nearer and nearer to his house. 'You don't want to do this,' she tried.

'You're wrong. I've wanted to do this for a long time, and I know it's what you want too.'

Shock flared as she looked up at him. 'How can you possibly...?'

'Know what you want? Your body language has been giving you away all evening.'

The awful truth was plain. He thought she was still pining for Greg and needed his brand of distraction. Hot anger suffused her and she kicked and squirmed in his grasp. 'Let me go, damn you.'

At the door of his studio he stopped in the circle of light from the entrance. Setting her down, he pulled her into his arms, his mouth closing over hers. Her mind reeled and speech became a monumental effort. 'Why won't you leave me alone?' she managed in a choked whisper.

'I've tried, pity help me. You don't make it easy.'

Perhaps because she didn't want to, she recognised in the vestiges of her hold on sanity. He was only doing this to prove his mastery over her, since she refused to agree not to see Greg, and the thought ripped through her like a knife-thrust. Why couldn't he simply love her?

Was she simply too hard to love? Her own mother had been able to walk away from her. Even Greg had admitted to using her to avoid committing himself to Sandra. 'What is it with me?' she cried from the depths of her soul. 'Do I wear a sign inviting misuse?'

His fingers raked through her hair as he urged her head back until his searing gaze held her in thrall. 'Don't you know?' he rasped. 'It isn't misuse you invite, but something much more primeval.'

Something died inside her as she realised he thought of her as a temptress, too wantonly dangerous to leave alone with Greg. In spite of the knowledge, part of her wanted desperately the solace of his arms and the warmth of his kisses. When she was back in Perth it would be all she would have of him. Was it so wrong?

In the confusion of her thoughts she was unaware of cupping her hands behind his neck and trailing her fingers through the hair which curled on to his collar.

When his oath rent the air, she realised what she had invited but his mouth was already claiming hers. Fire tore through her veins as he continued the trail of kisses along her collarbone and down to the shadowed valley between her breasts.

Her will seemed paralysed as he reached for the side-opening of her halter and blazed a fresh trail of sensual destruction along the creamy mounds. Pleasure warred with pain inside her as a million 'if only's played a bewildering chorus through her mind.

She should stop this, she knew, but she loved him too much to deny herself the fruit of his love-making. No matter what he thought of her, she was doomed to care for him for all the tomorrows granted to her. She could at least show him with her body what he wouldn't let her put into words.

All the same, she endured a moment of panic when he swept her into strong arms and moved to carry her inside. Mia's photographs watched over this room. Perhaps they had even made love here. What was she doing settling for so much less?

But it was already too late, even if she had found the strength to tell him she had changed her mind. The knobbly covering of the couch teased her sensitive skin as he set her down. A faint salt tang reached her nostrils as a breeze blew in from the sea.

Swamped by so many sensory impressions, she felt in danger of drowning and instinctively she reached for Steed, knowing that his hold was her lifeline.

Her touch snapped his remaining restraint. With little regard for their value, he shed his clothes in swift, savage movements. When he reached for her top she drew a sharp breath and crossed her hands defensively over her breasts.

'It's a sin to hide such beauty,' he murmured throatily. Forcing her hands down to her sides, he slid the halter off and bent his head. When his teeth ravaged the first sensitive peak she thought she would faint. But oblivion was denied as he turned his attention to her other breast, driving her to the very brink of her endurance.

She withstood the exquisite assault on her senses for as long as she could before allowing a groan of capitulation to escape her lips. No matter how much she yearned to be strong, to deny him herself, she accepted how desperately she wanted what was about to happen. Yet her eyes ached with unshed tears as she hearkened to the 'if only's for one fleeting last time.

There was so much to regret, so much to wish for, but an orphan learned early the futility of wishing. No one ever got everything they wanted. Some never got anything they wanted. Wasn't it better to settle for what you could have?

She was unaware of the moisture beading her cheeks until Steed brushed it away with the back of his hand. 'Regrets already, Lin?'

Closing her eyes tightly, she shook her head. How could she regret a moment she wanted with all her soul? Wasn't it better to have loved and lost? She would know the answer tomorrow.

She forced her eyes open. In the lamplight Steed's skin gleamed like mahogany as he rested one knee on the edge of the couch, while his other leg straddled her trembling form. No part of her was sacred to him and she wanted to hide her face in consternation. No one had ever made her feel so gloriously wanton before.

Never before had she known herself to be capable of such uninhibited responses. She wouldn't allow herself to think it was Steed's expertise which drove her to such breathtaking heights. Surely some part of him cared for her, to evoke such abandon in her? His mastery was so irresistible that she could hardly contain the explosive feelings building and building inside her.

'Oh, Steed.'

She could not restrain her choked cry and she dug her fingernails heedlessly into his unyielding flesh as he carried her with him, beyond thought, beyond reason. The purity of it was heartbreakingly poignant, bringing tears to her eyes as his possession reached the ultimate peak.

It was only as the pulsing ache began to subside that she realised what she had done. Dear heaven, she had allowed him to make love to her without the slightest resistance. In one night she had confirmed everything he believed about her and worse. How could she face him or herself in the cold light of day?

She tensed, tremors convulsing her as he began to kiss her again, this time deeply, without the fiery passion which had preceded his lovemaking. Everything in her longed to return his kisses in full measure but she could no longer hide from the bitter truth, that he didn't love her and never would, not while the shadow of his late wife haunted his life.

He sensed her withdrawal. 'Are you all right?'

Hysterical laughter bubbled in her throat. She had never felt less all right in her entire life. But she couldn't admit it and endure his cynical amusement. Women like her were used to recreational sex, weren't they? Commitment had nothing to do with it. She choked back a sob. 'I'm fine.' Was that her voice, so brittle and amused, as if she had not a care in the world?

He swung his feet to the floor. 'Are you sure?'

'What do you want me to say? That I'm sorry we made love? All right, you're damned right I am.' Sorry that love had so little to do with it, a tortured inner voice added.

If she stayed in this room a moment longer, she would tell him so. It would take so little for everything to come spilling out, both her shame at what she had permitted him to do to her and the love which had driven her to allow it. What a weapon he would have then. She didn't think she could bear his rejection after such an admission.

Unable to trust herself with him a moment longer, she cast around for her clothes and bundled them on then slammed out of the studio and up to her room.

Steed still hadn't come up by the time she finished throwing her things into a suitcase. What was she expecting? An apology? He thought he'd done her a favour, assuaging her *frustrations*. He couldn't know how many new ones he'd created and none of them had anything to do with Greg Iamil. That honour was entirely reserved for Steed alone.

Next morning there was still no sign of him as she lugged her case down to the jetty. It was too early for Ernest's regular run to the mainland but waiting in the boat-house was preferable to the nervous strain of hanging around the house knowing that Steed could walk in at any moment.

She heard Ernest pottering in his boat at the end of the jetty. Her suitcase was already aboard so he must be waiting for her to join him. Her feet dragged as she covered the short distance.

In the shadow of the jetty the caretaker was fiddling with the outboard motor, his back turned, but he grunted a greeting.

She went into the cabin to spare herself the sight of the island retreating in the distance but the sounds of their progress out to sea were equally heart-rending. They had been under way for ten minutes before she summoned the courage to go out on deck.

'I wondered how long it would take for you to surface,' drawled the last voice she had expected to hear.

Her knees buckled and she collapsed on to a banquette, shocked by the sight of Steed at the tiller, his expression unreadable under Ernest's broad-brimmed hat. 'You,' she seethed. 'Didn't you do enough damage last night?'

'I made sure there wouldn't be any babies,' he said smoothly.

'Of course not. Your plans don't include lasting relationships, do they?'

His hard gaze bored into her. 'Should they?'

'Not on my account.' Her pride wouldn't permit
her to give any other answer.

'So even if I propose to you, you won't come
back to the island with me?'

Was this some kind of test? 'Since it's unlikely
to happen, I won't dignify that with a response.'

'You are hurt, aren't you?'

It was so unexpected that she blinked back tears.
Hurting implies caring, which we both know isn't
an issue between us.'

'Then I must care for you very deeply, because
'm hurting like hell.'

Her limpid eyes lifted to him. 'But why? Because
ou felt you betrayed Mia?'

'What has Mia got to do with this? I wanted you,
Linden. I was driven to take you last night because
couldn't seem to reach you any other way. I admit
took advantage of your upset over Greg but...'

Her pained look flickered over him then out to
ea. 'You think I made love with you because Greg
ot married?'

'Didn't you?'

'God, no. I...' She closed her mouth on the
amning admission.

'You what? Say, it, Linden. Or shall I say it for
oth of us? I love you, more than I ever thought
was possible to love any woman. If you hadn't
un away, I'd have told you last night.'

'I was ashamed of how I behaved yesterday,' she
dmitted in a barely audible tone. 'I thought I'd
onfirmed your worst fears about me.'

He gave a muffled oath. 'Never be ashamed of
hat you have to give. Never. The only fears I con-

firmed last night were my own—that my caveman
tactics had driven you away.'

'I ran out because I thought all we had was sex,'
she confessed. 'I was so sure it was all you wanted.'

'Because it was what I tried to make myself believe.' His rueful smile flashed briefly. 'I'd told
myself you were a shameless gold-digger for so long
that I didn't want to admit I could be wrong.'

Hope fluttered inside her like a trapped bird.
'What made you change your mind?'

Pain gleamed briefly in his dark gaze. 'The way
you went after Jason without a thought for
yourself.'

She gestured dismissively. 'Anyone would have
done the same.'

'Kitty didn't. You didn't even hesitate. Then last
night when Greg offered to publish your book you
turned him down and sent him back to Sandra with
his tail between his legs.'

She gave a self-deprecating chuckle. 'You heard
all that?'

'Every word, even though you tried to make me
think you were considering his offer.'

'I wasn't,' she conceded softly.

'Then why didn't you admit it?'

Her molten gaze went to him. 'Because it would
have been too blatant an admission of my true
feelings.'

He slipped a rope over the tiller and moved carefully until he shared a bench with her. His nearness
was intoxicating and she felt her heartbeat quicken.
'What were you afraid of, Lin?'

'Finding out that you couldn't love me in return.'
She covered her face with her hands. 'I thought
you still loved Mia.'

The planes and angles of his face suddenly
sharpened. 'Mia killed any love I had for her long
before she died. Ours was a bright, shining passion
kindled in an instant in the Philippines. We took
precautions but she became pregnant with Jason,
so we married and I brought her here to live.'

Linden's breath caught in her throat. 'What went
wrong?' she forced herself to ask.

'At first she loved it all, my work, the attention.
But she missed the bright lights. She began to arrange her own social life whenever I was away. She
wasn't happy unless she had a crowd of admirers
around her, preferably male ones.'

Understanding came with a painful rush. 'And
you thought I was cut from the same cloth, didn't
you?'

'After I saw you with Greg, I was sure. Your enthusiasm for the outback could be just as fleeting
as Mia's was. I kept waiting for you to reveal your
true colours... and you never did.'

'You were waiting for the wrong colours,' she
said, her throat tight with love for him. 'Oh, Steed.'
So she had been right about Mia's affecting his at-
titude towards love, but not in the way she'd
thought. No wonder he had reacted so badly to her
perceived dalliance with Greg. It reminded him too
strongly of Mia's betrayal.

'What about Kitty Barret?' she asked in a
strained voice.

'You saw me going into her cabin?' When she nodded he frowned. 'I thought I caught a glimpse of you on deck but you'd gone back to your cabin when I investigated. If you'd watched for two more minutes you'd have seen me come out of her cabin again. I may be good but I'm not *that* good.'

Her eyes danced as she thought of last night. 'I'm not sure I agree with you, but go on.'

'She wanted some luggage she'd stored in my cabin. I took it to her and by the time I'd put it down she was stretched out on her bunk stark naked.'

Knowing Kitty as Linden did, the tactic was easy to imagine. 'What did you do?'

His smile was cynical. 'I could make you suffer the way I've suffered thinking you were in love with Greg, but I won't. I did what any gentleman would have done—bid her a pleasant goodnight and walked out as if nothing were amiss.'

'She must have been furious.'

'Spitting chips,' he confirmed. 'She couldn't believe I could resist her nubile charms. She forgot that I was already engaged to you.'

A shadow darkened Linden's features. 'Not for real, though.'

'It was more real than even I imagined. It sure explains why I wanted to murder Greg Hamil whenever I saw you with him.'

'Greg and I weren't lovers,' she insisted. 'He spent a few nights observing at the sleep centre, but that's all.'

'Which proves my point—the man's a fool,' he growled.

'You can't have it both ways,' she teased, gladness taking wing within her.

There was no mistaking the passion which kindled in his gaze. 'Murdering him is still a possibility until I get my ring safely on your finger and my baby inside you for good measure.'

The thought of bearing his child speared her with a longing so intense, it was like a physical pain. 'How will Jason cope with a real engagement? He reacted badly when Kitty suggested we might marry.'

'He was caught off-guard. After I assured him that you aren't trying to displace his mother, he began to like the idea of a stepmother. Apparently you play a pretty fair computer game.' He pulled her closer, his arms so tight around her that she could barely breathe. 'I don't want a replacement for Mia, Linden. I love you for yourself and I want us to be married as soon as possible.'

'It's what I want too, more than anything in the world.' Her voice was a throaty murmur above the lapping of the waves against the side of the boat.

'Then I'd better turn this boat around.' But he made no move to release the tiller. Instead he urged her backwards until she lay along the banquette, his body covering hers. Her eyes flared as his arousal became shockingly apparent.

'Steed, we can't, not out here.'

His persuasive caresses gave the lie to her denial. Warmth flooded her limbs as she opened to his demands with all the love in her soul. 'Well, maybe we can,' she amended, knowing it would be some time before they returned to the island. What did it matter? Everything her heart desired was here. In Steed's arms she would always be at home.

HARLEQUIN®

Don't miss these Harlequin favorites by some of our most
distinguished authors!
And now, you can receive a discount by ordering two or more titles!

HT#25645	THREE GROOMS AND A WIFE by JoAnn Ross	$3.25 U.S. $3.75 CAN.	☐
HT#25647	NOT THIS GUY by Glenda Sanders	$3.25 U.S. $3.75 CAN.	☐
HP#11725	THE WRONG KIND OF WIFE by Roberta Leigh	$3.25 U.S. $3.75 CAN.	☐
HP#11755	TIGER EYES by Robyn Donald	$3.25 U.S. $3.75 CAN.	☐
HR#03416	A WIFE IN WAITING by Jessica Steele	$3.25 U.S. $3.75 CAN.	☐
HR#03419	KIT AND THE COWBOY by Rebecca Winters	$3.25 U.S. $3.75 CAN.	☐
HS#70622	KIM & THE COWBOY by Margot Dalton	$3.50 U.S. $3.99 CAN.	☐
HS#70642	MONDAY'S CHILD by Janice Kaiser	$3.75 U.S. $4.25 CAN.	☐
HI#22342	BABY VS. THE BAR by M.J. Rodgers	$3.50 U.S. $3.99 CAN.	☐
HI#22382	SEE ME IN YOUR DREAMS by Patricia Rosemoor	$3.75 U.S. $4.25 CAN.	☐
HAR#16538	KISSED BY THE SEA by Rebecca Flanders	$3.50 U.S. $3.99 CAN.	☐
HAR#16603	MOMMY ON BOARD by Muriel Jensen	$3.50 U.S. $3.99 CAN.	☐
HH#28885	DESERT ROGUE by Erine Yorke	$4.50 U.S. $4.99 CAN.	☐
HH#28911	THE NORMAN'S HEART by Margaret Moore	$4.50 U.S. $4.99 CAN.	☐

(limited quantities available on certain titles)

	AMOUNT	$
DEDUCT:	10% DISCOUNT FOR 2+ BOOKS	$
ADD:	POSTAGE & HANDLING	$
	($1.00 for one book, 50¢ for each additional)	
	APPLICABLE TAXES*	$_____
	TOTAL PAYABLE	$_____
	(check or money order—please do not send cash)	

To order, complete this form and send it, along with a check or money order for the
total above, payable to Harlequin Books, to: **In the U.S.:** 3010 Walden Avenue,
P.O. Box 9047, Buffalo, NY 14269-9047; **In Canada:** P.O. Box 613, Fort Erie, Ontario,
L2A 5X3.

Name: _____

Address: _____ City: _____

State/Prov.: _____ Zip/Postal Code: _____

*New York residents remit applicable sales taxes.
  Canadian residents remit applicable GST and provincial taxes.
Look us up on-line at: http://www.romance.net

HBACK-JM4

Harlequin Romance ®
brings you

BABY BOOM

We are proud to announce the birth of our new bouncing baby series—Baby Boom!

Each month in 1997 we'll be bringing you your very own bundle of joy—a cute, delightful romance by one of your favorite authors. Our heroes and heroines are about to discover that two's company and three (or four...or five) is a family!

This exciting new series is all about the true labor of love...

Parenthood, and how to survive it!

Watch for:
#3443 *THREE LITTLE MIRACLES*
by Rebecca Winters

Tracey couldn't forget the devastating secret that had forced her to run out on Julien Chappelle four days after their honeymoon. What she hadn't counted on was that her brief marriage had left more than memories. A set of adorable triplets who needed their mom to come home! It seemed Tracey had only one motive for leaving, and three reasons to stay....

Available in February wherever Harlequin books are sold.

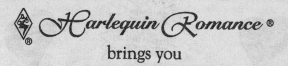

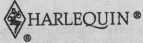

Heartbreak RANCH

Four generations of independent women…
Four heartwarming, romantic stories of the West…
Four incredible authors…

Fern Michaels
Jill Marie Landis
Dorsey Kelley
Chelley Kitzmiller

Saddle up with Heartbreak Ranch, an outstanding
Western collection that will take you on a whirlwind
trip through four generations and the exciting,
romantic adventures of four strong women who
have inherited the ranch from Bella Duprey,
famed Barbary Coast madam.

Available in March,
wherever Harlequin books are sold.

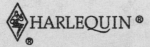

HARLEQUIN ®

Weddings by DeWilde

Since the turn of the century the elegant and fashionable
DeWilde stores have helped brides around the world
turn the fantasy of their "Special Day" into reality. But now the
store and three generations of family are torn apart by the
separation of Grace and Jeffrey DeWilde. Family members
face new challenges and loves in this fast-paced, glamorous,
internationally set series. For weddings and romance, glamour
and fun-filled entertainment, enter the world of DeWildes....

Watch for *ROMANCING THE STONES*,
by Janis Flores
Coming to you in February, 1997

Nick Santos was so close to solving the mystery of
the missing DeWilde jewels that he could almost taste it.
But Kate DeWilde was proving to be a major glitch in his
progress. And falling for his boss's daughter had put a
definite crimp in his investigative style. Doing as she asked
would probably mean kissing the case of a lifetime goodbye....

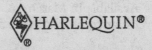

HARLEQUIN®

Look us up on-line at: http://www.romance.net

WBD11